The Wife; or, Caroline Herbert

Maria Susanna Cooper

THE WIFE;

OR,

CAROLINE HERBERT.

BY THE LATE AUTHOR

OF THE

"EXEMPLARY MOTHER."

1813

VOLUME I

LETTER I.

To Miss Herbert.

Bath, — — — — —

YOU will be surprised, my dear Lucia, to receive a letter from me, dated Bath. Amongst the number of vagaries, (may I be permitted so to call them?) with which my good aunt has been lately possessed, this last has afforded me the greatest pleasure. She is one of the most whimsical of human beings, and it would be shocking indeed if some of her whims were not agreeable. How could my dear uncle entrust me to her guardianship?—But he, poor soul! was always under her direction.—He was never out of leading strings. I wonder she suffered him to take a trip to the other world; but her sublunary views were answered: witness the fine estate he bequeathed her, to which my ladyship has one day or other an undoubted right.

Since our arrival, nothing has been thought of but a proper adjustment of our lodgings to receive company. To rush from one extreme into another is the common failing of humourists. This strange being, this fantastic relative of mine, who lately could not bear a gleam of sunshine to penetrate into her apartment, now glows in the flaming reflection of scarlet furniture. To display the ornaments of her mind, she has been furnishing a library, though, to fill up vacancies, many of her authors are—neatly carved in wood! She, whose erudition never extended beyond a book of domestic cookery or some modern novel, now claims an external acquaintance, at least, with philosophers, historians, and poets. Well! defend me from the vanity of apparent wisdom, which will only serve to betray my own *folly!* Yet I too, perhaps, in a way very different from my aunt, am too fond of outward show. But men, who are charmed with a pleasing outside, do not expect much decoration within; while she, who only *affects* mental improvements, will be despised for her deficiencies.

My next letter perhaps will give you some account of my public amusements. My good aunt cannot yet exhibit her finery to the world;—but I assure you it has been drawn forth from her chest, examined, and re-examined, and new modelled. She has captivating charms to those who are votaries of Plutus, rather than of Cupid. Eighteen hundred pounds a year is a transporting sound to a young spendthrift, who has long heard nothing but the vociferation of duns. She might be assured of his care for the preservation of her life. I am afraid poor BEAUTY would find no modern Paris to decide the prize in her favour, if WEALTH came in competition. As to WISDOM, she is now a less formidable opponent than at the time of that important contest.

I must bid you adieu! my dear, as my aunt requires my attendance to an auction. I shall write as frequently as possible, without waiting for your regular answers, yet I earnestly wish for a letter from you. Mine will now be a busy life; may yours, my Lucy, be a happy one! and may you always continue to love

Your ever affectionate

CLARA WOODFORD.

LETTER II.

To Miss Herbert.

WELL! child, I have made my appearance in the streets, and in the Rooms.

I have been admired by

> "The grave and the gay
> The clown and the beau,"

envied by the young, and pitied by the ancient of my own sex. Think, my Lucy, what a series of delights Bath has afforded to one, who for several months had been entirely immured in a sick chamber. Before I appeared, Miss Somerton was the universal toast, but my radiance has thrown a shade on her lustre. Poor girl! I really pity her, and yet I cannot readily forego a single glance of admiration.

You will wish to know the characters of some of my *particular* admirers. You may see a thousand such buzzing insignificant beings in every place of public resort: Lord Monmouth is the most distinguished for birth and fortune, but in merit he has no pre-eminence. As to my good aunt, she plays away her precious moments at whist, and is as happy with a new party at cards, as her niece with a new admirer, or a good partner at a ball.

I believe I must give you a description of my first appearance. I had heard of Miss Somerton's conquests; I had seen her, and my little heart fluttered and exalted when I compared my own charms with hers in my looking glass, (the mirror of vanity, perhaps you'll say); so I resolved to burst forth in an effulgence of brightness. I made an elegant and resplendent appearance. I really was a very striking figure.—I paraded before a large glass several times. At last, just as I was stepping into the coach, a fit of humility seized me: surely I shall not become a foil to this Miss Somerton, thought I; and I stood in suspense some minutes whether to advance or retreat. Whilst this struggle passed in my mind, I was summoned down to my aunt's apartment, where an intimate of hers, with a beau son, and belle daughter, were equipped for the Rooms, and called upon me to make one of the party. A few well-timed compliments from the young man, raised my drooping spirits. The spark of vanity rekindled. I gave my hand to the flatterer, and my heart danced merrily to the sweet tune of adulation.

On entering the Rooms we found a numerous, splendid company, and I observed with a palpitation of delight, that my appearance excited a general buzz of admiration. Miss Somerton, who was surrounded by a gay circle, and addressed with all the unmeaning phrases of love's vocabulary, had the mortification of seeing herself forsaken by every admirer, and observed the homage paid to novelty in the person of Clara Woodford: for, my dear, vain as you may think me, I really believe novelty has more attractions than mere beauty. Pleased as I was with the incense, I was not particularly charmed with the person of any of my worshippers. To Lord Monmouth, as the most considerable in rank, I paid most attention. I felt an ill-natured pleasure in tracing the distress of Miss Somerton's heart in her countenance. She affected an indifference which betrayed her emotions. I joined for a time in the dance, and when I left the set, Lord Monmouth quitted Miss Somerton to join my party. She pretended to be oppressed with excessive heat, and placed herself in a distant corner. O, my dear, what envious, deceitful creatures we are! Miss Somerton's head involuntarily turned towards us; then with a malicious titter, she whispered a young lady who sate beside her, lifting up her eyes and hands as if in amazement at my behaviour. Own, my dear Lucy, that it required prodigious strength of mind to support such an exaltation without giddiness,—my brain was light—it turned round—my tongue was uncommonly voluble, and my eyes, I believe, sparkled with added lustre. Lord Monmouth and the other beaux addressed me with every complimentary expression which the language of flattery could furnish. I thought myself a superior being, and am yet scarcely reconciled to the common occurrences of life: however, my Lucy, though surrounded by admirers, and elated with triumphs, my friendship for you is ever lively. What can be the reason of your silence? I am very anxious to know the state of your family. Is your brother married to Miss Berkeley? I am half angry, but more apprehensive. My heart is deeply interested in every circumstance relative to you, and I am ever

most tenderly yours,

CLARA WOODFORD.

LETTER III.

To Miss Berkeley.

COULD I ever have believed that I should have taken up my pen with unwillingness to address the dearest, and most excellent of her sex? Alas! It is in an agony of distress that I write. I must renounce you; I must resign the hopes nearest my heart. You never, never can be mine. To save my father, I sacrifice that fortune which I vainly wished to share with you. Alas! I must renounce the beloved of my soul!

The generosity of his spirit, and some taste for expense have involved him in difficulties from which it is in my power to extricate him. Whilst I enjoy the glorious privilege of paying the debt of filial gratitude, my heart is rent by its own, and, (may I not say likewise?) with your anguish. Yes, my amiable Caroline, (permit me once more, and for the *last* time to call you *mine!*) It is not vanity, but a perfect knowledge of your sentiments, that influences me to believe you will participate in the grief which overwhelms me.—You would not have promised your hand to a man to whom you had not given your heart.—Continue to bless me with your esteem, and pity me in the painful triumph of duty over love. Alas! we must not meet till I am more resigned to my fate— till I can cease to love you with that inexpressible tenderness of affection, which now actuates the heart of

Your most devoted

CHARLES HERBERT.

LETTER IV.

To Miss Woodford.

BY your accusations of me, my dear friend, for my continued silence, I find you are ignorant of the misfortunes of our family. Grief, shame, and filial duty, prevented me from disclosing the sad secret. But it can no longer be concealed.—Alas! it is too well known, and I owe to your tender solicitude every particular of our unhappy story.

My father's turn for *pleasure* (a term much too mild for irregularities which reason and religion condemn), involved him in the greatest difficulties. To relieve himself from them, he hazarded at the gaming table the shattered remains of his fortune. He lost *more* than all. He was soon after arrested for some just debts, and carried to a spunging house.—I was then on a visit in Kent—My brother was also from home, yet not at such a distance but that he received early intelligence of the disastrous event. Judge of his affliction! He flew to the place of my father's confinement. O what a spectacle! My poor father, weakened by repeated excesses, had been unable to bear the shock with tolerable fortitude—He sunk under it—Even his senses were affected.—Tears and exclamations somewhat relieved his oppressed heart. My brother observing the perturbation of his mind, intreated him to compose himself, and promised to contrive a means for his deliverance.—The unhappy parent only shook his head, and gave himself up to fruitless lamentations on his folly. Fatigued, however, by his own exertions, sleep at length, insensibly weighed down his weary eye-lids.

During this desirable forgetfulness, my brother revolved in his mind what resolution it became him to take. Every thing was adjusted for his marriage with Miss Berkeley:—He felt as a lover, but he still more severely suffered as a son. By the sale of the estate, bequeathed to him by his grandmother, which was to be settled on the intended Mrs. Herbert, he knew he could release the wretched prisoner, whose numerous debts required no smaller sacrifice for his discharge. Alas! *I* have nothing to offer—my small fortune, with my brother's expected patrimony—are all lost in the general wreck. My father wanted immediate succour. No remedy presented itself but an application to our relation, Mr. Millar. That gentleman's ample fortune would permit him to spare a more considerable sum without any security for repayment; but my brother was as little disposed to solicit, as the other to grant such a favour. He resigned the hope of obtaining Miss Berkeley's hand; but, gracious heaven! how severe was the trial!

My father awaked somewhat refreshed, and his spirits less agitated. My brother, with a tender embrace, intreated him to be comforted, told him he believed he had contrived the means for his release; but if his expectation failed him in this attempt, he would not sleep till he had by some mode or other, procured his enlargement. The effect this assurance produced on my father, was a revival of all those generous sentiments which had so long lain dormant in his breast; he aggravated his own errors, and when he considered that his wretched situation might be injurious to his son's happiness, he beat his bosom in self-upbraiding anguish.

In the mean time, the servants having heard of my father's arrest hastened to communicate it to me. I can only say, my grief was equal to my brother's. I returned immediately to town, and hastened to this wretched parent. What contrition and despair were visible in his countenance! I have before confessed to you that I have sometimes, and perhaps too warmly, blamed his extravagance: my brother has thought my interference improper, and my solicitude severe. I acknowledge my fault, and I assure you as soon as I heard of his imprisonment, tender commiseration, sympathizing affection, took entire possession of my soul. Good God! to see him pale,—emaciated—weeping,—to hear him *condemn himself,*—almost *deify my brother,* and supplicate forgiveness from us both, who could feel any other emotions than those of the tenderest commiseration?—I received your letter at this time. You desired an immediate answer. But could I attend to your request when my mind was all confusion? My father's hurry of spirits brought on a fever which has reduced him so low, that his recovery is doubtful.

* * * * *

God be praised! he is somewhat better this morning. My brother's fortitude is amazing: he has acquainted Miss Berkeley with his resolution: he has given up his fond hopes, and protests he will not involve her in his distress.

I will write again as soon as possible, for I know you will take an interest in our wretchedness, both from your natural sensibility, and from your sincere attachment to

Your affectionate and

unhappy Friend,

LUCIA HERBERT.

LETTER V.

To Miss Woodford.

WHAT scenes have I to relate! My brother has actually treated with Mr. Millar about the sale of his estate, and this very evening they agreed to meet to settle preliminaries.

With unshaken fortitude has he submitted to the severity of his fate. I condoled with him on the dreadful necessity—I applauded his greatness of mind.

"My Lucia," said he, "I only perform my duty. I pursue the dictates of filial love, and I rely on Providence to support me under distress, or to relieve me from it. I suffer inexpressible pangs, not only for my own disappointment of the most delightful expectations, but for the distress which I fear I have occasioned in the breast of the most excellent of women: yet religion, while it enables her to sympathise with me, will also inculcate on my heart the lesson of resignation."

Just as he had pronounced these words, the door opened, and two ladies rushed in. They were Mrs. and Miss Berkeley. The latter eagerly gazed on my brother for some moments, then bursting into tears, "O! Mr. Herbert!" said she, "could you determine to abandon me for ever? Or rather, did you harbour a fear that I could forsake you?"

My brother's eyes were fixed on the ground, his cheeks, which had been crimsoned with joy on her entrance, were now overspread with paleness; and it was some time before the emotions struggling in his breast would allow him to find utterance for his feelings. At last, with unusual agitation, he exclaimed, "O my Caroline, why did you visit me at such a crisis? I am the willing victim of filial duty; but your presence will unfit me for the sacrifice. It recalls the idea of the delights I must forego; of the happiness I had promised myself in your arms. But it must not be; honour and affection forbid the thought. Bless with your love some other" —

He could proceed no farther; but threw himself into a chair in breathless grief. Mrs. Berkeley was extremely affected; "I have long considered you, Sir," said she, "as my son; have you in any instance forfeited my good opinion; and shall I lose the happiness of such an addition to my family, because you have lessened your fortune, by improving your virtue? I thank Heaven our circumstances do not require such a sacrifice. How could you apprehend, my dear Sir, you should lose my daughter by saving your father? Know us better, sir: Caroline is yours: I join your hands. If we loved you before this exalted conduct, we now reverence and esteem you more than we can express."

"And who," exclaimed Miss Berkeley, "would not willingly resign wealth, to obtain a satisfaction which its accumulation cannot bestow? Talk not, dear Mr. Herbert, of an inevitable separation. Your father's debts are discharged. My heart has long been your's. I consider myself as affianced to you by solemn promises. Have you not then a right to share my fortune? And how can a portion of it be better employed, than in restoring the peace of such a family, of which I consider myself as a part? I glory in my choice; and my mother's approbation sanctifies it."

Then turning to me, she added, "I beg your pardon, my dear Lucia, if I have seemed to neglect you. I know the whole of your sad story. Think you we will permit our sister to suffer from deficiencies, it is in our power to supply?"

"Come," said Mrs. Berkeley, "come, my Lucy, and join with us in persuading your brother to be just to himself, and to make us all happy."

I was too much affected to answer otherwise, than by tears. My brother gazed on Miss Berkeley, with looks, which shewed his purpose was suspended. Perceiving his irresolution, and that it depended on him to pronounce the happiness or misery of both—"Can you hesitate, my dear brother," said I, "when Miss Berkeley permits you to make her happy?"

His cheeks glowed with the warmth of his feelings. "O," cried he at last, "I am so circumstanced, that I am fearful the gratification of my love, would be the forfeiture of her esteem." — "No," interrupted she, "on the contrary, my esteem would be increased, by the correspondence of our sentiments. I should then have it in my power to say, had I been in the same distress, Mr. Herbert would have considered, that those whose hearts are in union, can have no separate interests."

My brother could resist no longer. In an extacy of tender emotion, he caught her willing hand, and exclaimed, "Most amiable of women! when I examine my own heart, these pleas are unanswerable. O, my Caroline! words cannot describe my sensations! — My mother too," — turning to Mrs. Berkeley, who affectionately embraced him. "Ah, how much am I indebted to both!"

My tears spoke my gratitude. Mrs. Berkeley hung over the happy lovers, and blessed them. I was all transport. — It was judged prudent that I should prepare my father for this unexpected change. I did so with all the caution in my power, yet the joyful surprise overcame him, and he fainted in my arms. The meeting between him and my brother, was almost insupportably affecting, and when, at my father's desire, he was introduced to Mrs. and Miss Berkeley, his acknowledgements were too self-abasing for their generosity.

As to myself, my debt of gratitude is immense — Miss Berkeley insists on presenting me with £ 3000. on the day of her marriage. She saw me struggling for utterance. My eyes were more eloquent than my lips. "Why," resumed she, taking my hand, "why, my Lucy, this agitation? Are we not all one family? Or, perhaps," continued she, with a smile, "you think I assume a right of disposal, which does not now belong to me. But your brother and I are actuated by one mind. — Look not grave, my beloved sister, nor put on this face of obligation. — You would have acted thus, had I been in your place. Not a word more on the subject." My dear, dear sister! was all I could *say*: but ah! what do I *feel*!

From this delightful re-union, my father declares, he dates his returning health. I cannot say his looks are altered for the better, but he is in good spirits, and tells us, he shall be perfectly well when my brother's happiness is completed. The ceremony is to be performed next week. I shall have no time to write, till that is over.

How does your aunt? what is your present situation? have you yet had any regular attacks upon your heart, or is it all general incense offered to your vanity? write as soon, and as often as possible.

I am, my Clara,

your's most affectionately,

LUCIA HERBERT.

LETTER VI.

To Miss Herbert.

INDEED, my dear, I do most sincerely share your pains and pleasures. I admire and reverence your brother. I am charmed with Miss Berkeley, and as to Mrs. Berkeley, she is the paragon of old ladies and of mothers—passive obedience, and non-resistance to such a parent, must be the very acmè of a child's ambition. I most cordially rejoice at the happy conclusion of this threatening affair. May every scene of these lovers' future lives open to them new prospects of happiness, as extensive as their virtues!

I am still excessively admired and caressed; but as to particular devoirs, you are too *particular*, child, in your enquiries. "'Tis time enough yet, 'Tis time enough yet."

Let me know every circumstance about the wedding. These excellent people must enjoy life. I suppose they will be perfect patterns of every connubial virtue, such as we shall gaze at till our eyes ache, and our hearts despond. Pardon me, Lucy, for including you—you are a very good young woman; the aching eye, the desponding heart, will therefore be the sole property of

your giddy, but truly affectionate,

CLARA WOODFORD.

LETTER VII.

To Miss Woodford.

MY DEAR CLARA,

I HAVE received your friendly congratulations. My brother and Miss Berkeley were on Wednesday last united in indissoluble bonds. A day, which imparted happiness to all around them. Mrs. Berkeley's joy was pure and unmixt, but my father's was blended with an humiliating remembrance. He blessed the amiable pair with the utmost tenderness; he gazed upon them till his eyes betrayed the emotions of his heart. Every day since that happy one, his looks have visibly altered for the worse; and this morning, when we went into his chamber to pay our duty to him, we found him in bed. My brother flew to him, and inquired how he felt, with eagerness. My father could not return him an immediate answer; but he gave him a strenuous embrace.

Soon after, in tremulous accents, he said, "My child, my preserver! your guilty father dies a victim to his own vices, contrasted with the virtues of his son. My heart is broken!—Nothing, but the desire of securing your immediate happiness, could have animated me to support the appearance of health and chearfulness. That desire is accomplished, and I submit without a murmur, to the avenging hand of a just Providence. A few days, my son, a very few days, will release me from my present sufferings, but consign me, alas! I fear to future misery."

Here he clasped his hands in agony. My brother, and sister, and myself, threw ourselves on our knees beside him, in speechless sorrow.—After a melancholy pause, my dear father continued—"Do not grieve for me, my children; for me, whose faulty conduct would have destroyed your temporal happiness, had not this excellent woman saved us. With what regret do I look back on a life of dissipation! Alas! alas! had I improved time, I should have enjoyed eternity. I do, I own I do, dread the pangs of dissolution, but these will be of short duration, compared with those I am condemned to suffer.—Never-ceasing misery must be the portion of the unworthy husband—the cruel father!"

"Forbear, dear sir," interrupted my brother; "you wound us deeply, by this severe retrospect of your actions. Who has lived free from errors? You have seen, condemned, and determined in future, to avoid a repetition of yours. Spare us, my father, oh! spare yourself this painful recrimination. You have been the means, not of destroying, but of hastening our happiness, and will you, by indulging despondency, be the occasion of our misery?"

He was proceeding with a tender anxiety, when we perceived that my father had fainted. His servant entering, assisted us in recovering him, and with tears, told us, that his master had several times been very ill, but would not permit him to mention these attacks, lest the apprehensions of his approaching death should occasion a delay of my brother's marriage. O let us hope, that so affectionate a heart must be sincerely and acceptably penitent!

It was some time before my poor father revived, and when he did, he desired us to leave him, that he might, if possible, compose himself to sleep.

Such, my dear, is our present state. How dreadful a reverse! I must lay down my pen—O, may I resume it with a pleasing hope.

* * * *

Alas! My Clara, we bid adieu to hope! my father sent for us all to his chamber again, last night, and we found him much weaker than before. "My dear son," said he, "I am going very fast. I dread to part from you all, but my greatest fear is,—that we shall never meet again. How differently do the pleasures of this world appear, when reviewed on a death bed, from that alluring representation which we form of them in the hour of health.—O, that I had always beheld them in their true light. If even venial transgressions are alarming, because destructive of the purposes of life, how dreadful is it to reflect on the commission of heinous offences! how many actions, which I ranked amongst my virtues, appear on a death-bed, in all the dark deformity of vice!—And, ah! how hideous every error!—O, take heed to preserve that delightful consciousness, which only can secure you "peace at the last." But you, my children, want not these admonitions. Your past lives are the best lesson for your future improvement.—Yet—do not presume on your own strength, lest presumption prove your ruin.—*Trust in* your Maker and Redeemer!—*May* GOD *preserve you*!—I grow faint—Adieu! my beloved children."—He then sunk down in his bed, faint and speechless.

* * * *

Our grief is inexpressible. My amiable sister endears herself still more to us, by her sensibility on this occasion. My brother and she, sit on one side of the bed; Mrs. Berkeley and I, take our places on the other. My poor father lies dozing almost continually.—He sometimes starts from his sleep—looks on us all—moves his lips—and then lifts his eyes to heaven.

Adieu! my dear. I can write no more at present.

* * * *

O! Miss Woodford! my dear father has breathed his last!—After two days and nights continual watchings and anxiety, during which he remained dozing or speechless, he started from his sleep, and caught hold of poor old Stanley, his servant, who sate bathed in tears, on a chair by his bed side.—He gazed wildly on us all for some moments.—At length, with tolerable composure, he exclaimed—"Farewell! my dear children.—Be religious, and you must be—happy." He then fell back on his pillow, and expired immediately.

My tears will not permit me to write more.

* * * *

I will endeavour to conclude my letter. My brother and sister, though deeply affected, bear their loss like Christians. My dear father's remains were conveyed yesterday to their last awful receptacle.—Merciful GOD! grant that his errors may be forgiven, and his penitence accepted!

We shall very soon leave London. Mrs. Berkeley, who never enjoyed her health in town, finds it very much injured by the close confinement and anxiety she has lately suffered, and thinks it necessary to go into the country as soon as possible. My brother and sister will accompany her, and she insists on my making her house my home, till my brother can purchase one, for I believe he intends to be in town only a month or two in the winter. He will be a father to me. Ah! with whom can I be so happy, as with him and my sister? We are united by the strictest bonds of friendship. We mingle our tears, and enjoy a sadly-pleasing sympathy of sorrow. The same motives of consolation raise us above the afflictions of mortality. My sister, like a guardian angel, teaches us acquiescence in the will of heaven, and

"Truths divine come mended from her tongue."

Her religion is perfectly rational; entirely free from enthusiasm and bigotry. It dictates an universal benevolence.

I hope to have a letter from you, as soon as we get into Hampshire, and let me, among the blessings still preserved to me, continue to enjoy that friendship with which you have hitherto favoured

Your sincerely affectionate,

LUCIA HERBERT.

LETTER VIII.

To Miss Herbert.

WHAT has your amiable family suffered! I cannot express the anguish I felt on reading your letter.—At such a time too—so melancholy a gloom overclouding such delightful prospects!—dreadful indeed! yet the trial calls you to the exercise of superior virtues: and your own reflections will afford you the sweetest consolation. You are most sublime mortals. I tremble at my own reptile littleness, when I contemplate your eagle flights, yet I do not find my power over hearts at all in the wane. The adorable Clara Woodford, is the universal toast. I lead the dance—I direct the music—I am the soul of every diversion. But I am afraid I could not support misfortune with your fortitude, nor properly fill the part so admirably sustained by Mrs. Herbert. You have been called forth to great occasions. Tell me, how these exalted beings act in the common occurrences of life? Can they descend to domestic concerns? My admiration and my curiosity are both awake, and you know the natural impatience of

your affectionate and truly

sympathising,

CLARA WOODFORD.

LETTER IX.

To Miss Woodford.

THOUGH in the midst of the amusements of the gay fashionable world, you assure me you wait with impatience for a letter. Can a description of the calm scenes of domestic life, a picture of unfashionable, connubial happiness, please so universally-admired a toast.—Yes, my dear Miss Woodford, you have too much good sense to be *infatuated* with the syren song of flattery, though for a while, you are rather lulled by its influence.

Do not think me guilty of affectation nor envy, when I tell you that I prefer the society of this excellent family, to all your boasted pleasures; and yet, my dear, I can easily account for your transient elation of heart, on such extensive triumphs. But I pity the victim of your charms, poor Miss Somerton, and think it possible (do not be displeased, my Clara!) that a similar fate may soon be your's. In a place where there is such a quick succession of new faces, even superior beauty may be deserted. Indeed your own observation dictated by *some* share of humility, (unless you meant it in general, and not to extend to particulars,) will, I hope, prepare you for the natural consequence of sudden and vehement admiration. The hearts of these modern gallants, are too constantly devoted to self-complacence, to be long capable of other attachments. But I will say no more on this subject, lest you should suspect my observations to be rather the result of envy, than of friendship.

My brother and sister are the most rationally-happy couple, I ever knew. Every day brings with it an increase of tenderness; yet this, so far from lessening their attention to religious duties, serves as an additional motive to invigorate their performance of them, as the only lasting basis on which to perpetuate each other's esteem. I did not believe it possible to lead a life of perfect innocence, to preserve an uniform chearfulness, till I observed my sister's every action. Even my brother, I doubt, must yield to her in sanctity of sentiment. Every action of her life, may be considered as an address to God. I never before beheld such sweetness of disposition, as is displayed in her behaviour. She blends Christian fortitude, with more than maternal tenderness of heart. Meekness and charity, are the inmates of her gentle breast. She understands and practises every domestic duty.

With what exquisite tenderness does she sooth the infirmities of age! Every filial attention, every benevolent office, is discharged with an alacrity that supplies her with health and spirits. What would I give to possess half her virtues! I believe I shall be the maiden aunt of the family, for I should not be satisfied with a less degree of happiness that these good people enjoy, and yet I ought to expect less, as I possess such an inferior degree of merit. But so it is; however this is to be considered, that I have not seen the man for whose sake I would wish to exchange the name of

your affectionate

LUCIA HERBERT.

The Wife; or, Caroline Herbert

LETTER X.

To Miss Herbert.

NEVER was there a truer prophet! You are quite a Cassandra, my dear, and gained as little belief till your prophecy was verified. My reign lasted but five weeks, six hours, and fifty minutes, and then a usurper assumed the government, and I was deposed. I was shocked at this revolution. High treason deserves to be punished with the loss of these rebels' heads, but the misfortune is, these creatures have no heads to lose. You perhaps suspect their having no hearts. We can only judge of causes from effects, and the latter are so pleasing in the self-consequence and worldly importance they give us, that one is unwilling to be deceived as to the former. But I must be more serious, for the matter I am entering upon requires me to be so.

I have a lover, and such a lover as will excite your envy in the superlative degree: I judge you by the comparative. If you call this an insinuation, I plead guilty.—Now, for the lover. I imagine then a lover, with all the youth of Ganymede, the liveliness and agility of Mercury, the wit and grace of Apollo, the courage, without the impetuosity, of Achilles, the beauty, without the effeminacy, of Paris, (I believe this is what the critics call an anti-climax, for I should have began with heroes, and then ascended to the deities, but no matter,) well then, you must imagine all these, and you will have an idea of— a perfect contrast to my lover. O! child, that I could borrow a little of the Promethean art, and breathe somewhat of soul into many unanimated forms that occupy a space in these regions of pleasure. As to my swain, in serious truth, he shines with all the resplendent advantages of golden lustre. He is an eminent merchant, who has accumulated the sum of fifty thousand pounds. Is not this a capital recommendation? To my aunt, I assure you, it is, for it seems to absorb every disqualifying circumstance. She considers only

What pleasures will abound

When I've got £ 50,000!

The line is not harmonious, but the subject matter she thinks most delightful music. Whereas I think less of what abounds, than of what is deficient. And O! my dear, here are so many articles, that I know not where to make an imprimis.—His features are distorted, his person is awkward and ungenteel, his manners are unpolished, and his mind is unprincipled: yet one item I must add, that he has no vice, inconsistent with a passion for money. Charming ingredients these for a husband! Even my vanity suggests to me that my fortune has made a deeper impression than my person or merit, on his heart; and that vanity is a powerful enemy to his address. What! to have the inanimate preferred to the animate! No, my dear, I will bear no such rival. The man is desirous of cultivating no other qualities in me than prudence and oeconomy, and these are scions which he must engraft from his own tree, if he would reap the fruits. To say the truth, I do not think the stock will bear them; it will still be a wilding.

Mr. Selden saw me on a visit. His looks, it is certain, betrayed some marks of discomposure, but he very carefully made enquiries whether the "goddess had aught to give" before he paid his adorations. On the information of my fortune he offered the incense of flattery; but that he worshipped the golden idol was very evident to my distinguishing faculties. He waited on my aunt, made his proposals in form, was accepted and introduced to Miss, that she might give her passive voice. The reptile would not take a denial. He attributed to modesty, the effects of dislike, and he admired me truly, for what he misinterpreted in his favour. What a sad thing it is not to have one's negative accepted!

My aunt is so much pleased with Mr. Selden, that she threatens me with the loss of her affection, unless I accept him for an husband. I protest she has my consent for her own marriage with him, without any conditions; and to whisper a hint in your ear, I have some thoughts of intreating Mr. Herbert to become my guardian, as Mr. Bennet, who married my cousin, is not enough a man to my taste for this charge.

I will soon acquaint you whether my aunt's perseverance in the affair, renders it necessary for my peace to take this step. If it be, exert your influence over your brother, and you will most highly oblige

your sincerely affectionate

CLARA WOODFORD.

LETTER XI.

To Charles Herbert, Esq.

THE first intelligence that greeted me on my arrival in England, was that of your nuptials. I was not surprised, Charles—I thought what all your preachments would end in. What a deal of time and pains have I thrown away upon you.—You were a tolerably idle boy at school. I had hopes of you.—At college you were somewhat of an amphibious animal: a relish for the pleasures of life was blended with a fear of its excesses. The documents of a sage father, and the lessons of a prudish mother, meeting with a disproportionate share of natural gravity, confined you within limits which you would in no wise pass. Poor Herbert! are you become indeed the married man? And how sit your chains upon you, Charles? Do you not wish that you had profited by my instructions? You have never read Lord Chesterfield's advice, if you married to live soberly. An adept in his system is bound by neither moral nor religious laws, but is a freethinker in opinion, and a libertine in principle and practice.

Will you let me know your real state? Are you happily coupled (Gods! can it be possible?) or miserably yoked? I have a regard for you, Charles—a long acquaintance—your attachment to me—your well meant, though hum-drum lectures, dispose me to feel a kind of tender pity for your weaknesses, and to be as much as ever your's

WILTON.

LETTER XII.

To Lord Wilton.

PLEASURE and pain were blended in my emotions on perusing your Lordship's letter. We have passed many chearful hours together. Each has endeavoured to convince the other. Each has failed. Why can I not congratulate you on the same circumstance, which is the source of my joy? I have been a truant from school, but never, never will I be a renegade from matrimony.

I wish, most devoutly wish, that I had been a more successful advocate with you in the cause of true happiness. Can you be such a sceptic as to doubt my felicity in my inviolable attachment to the most excellent of human beings? I have been chearful, I have been many times lively, but never was I perfectly happy till my Caroline's heart and hand became indissolubly mine.

You talk of chains. Ah! my Lord, it is the licentious mind that forges for itself the fetters of slavery.—My Caroline is the chosen of my soul. To oblige her, to pursue her inclination, is to walk in the path traced by the hand of providence. O, Lord Wilton! I had taken my last farewell of this incomparable woman. I had resigned my fortune to save a distressed father. I could not support the thought of my Caroline's being so nearly allied to poverty and misery. She released me from prison, she gave liberty to my father, and, oh! extatic condescension, she gave me, herself. Since my affliction on the death of that dear parent, I have not known a care. My Caroline is the promoter, and partaker of all my joys. She refines, she ennobles every gratification.

We are at present with Mrs. Berkeley, the worthy mother of the best of women. My sister accompanied us down, and will live with us. Their days flow on in an uninterrupted course of benevolent offices. Can you form any idea of our bliss? It is not in the power of words to delineate a perfect picture of the happiness of

your Lordship's

sincerely affectionate

CHARLES HERBERT.

LETTER XIII.

To Charles Herbert, Esq.

> "If thou be'st he, but ah! how fall'n, how changed
> From him" who in our happy childish days
> Was prompt in idleness.

YOUR letter, Herbert, resounding the praises of matrimony and Caroline, and Caroline and matrimony, was so much in alt, that upon my soul I could not compass it.—Not a note in unison with my feelings.—I read a little one day, laid aside the letter—took it again, another—it was then too near bed time, and operated as a soporific—in about a week I got to the end, but it never will bear a revisal.—Sure you have found with Nat. Lee, that

"There's a pleasure in being mad

Which none but madmen know."

I have no idea, I *can* have no idea of your sublimities. You soar above the clouds—but at present the novelty of your state attracts you. The recurrence of domestic concerns will act with a repulsive force. You fly temptation however I find—are shut up in the country. When will you emerge? I shall really be glad to meet you in town, and to see the spell broken which confines you within the matrimonial circle.

I am ever your's,

WILTON.

LETTER XIV.

To Miss Herbert.

"HAPPY, happy, happy pair!" I did not think, my dear, that my consent would have been followed so soon by the parties' approbation. I made my repulse in the most explicit terms. It was impossible to be mistaken. The man took it in dudgeon. He actually threatened revenge, and in the first emotions of his wrath, being soothed by my kind aunt, he made proposals that he should administer, and receive consolation. The old lady, who never expected, I suppose, to hear again the credentials of love, was so enlivened by the sound, that Despair, lately her companion, took her flight with PRUDENCE. I, who never had any acquaintance with the sage dame (Prudence, I mean, for my aunt has given up all title to the character of sapience) thought she had erected an impregnable fortress in the old dowager's heart. What was my surprise then, when I found she had surrendered without the least capitulation? The good lady, thinking she had no time to lose, commenced bride before her poor niece dreamt of the transition. How, I wonder, could I survive the shock of losing such a lover? I did however bear it most heroically: but the loss of the lover was not the only consideration.

The day after the ceremony, my aunt and new uncle gave me to understand that I had no farther favours to expect from them. "Well, madam," said I, since you have chosen a protector of your person, you'll permit me to appoint a guardian to my fortune, and to withdraw my person from those who have no right to detain it." "To Mr. Selden," answered she, ready to burst with passion, "as my husband, I can transfer my power. He will not abuse it. Indeed he had once a better opinion of you than you deserved." "I am glad, for your sake, madam," said I, "as well as my own, that he was an inconstant. You have found the 'way to win him,' I hope you have also learned the 'way to keep him.'"

I don't know, my dear, whether I do right in giving you this account of myself. Perhaps you will think a little more respect to my aunt would become me better; but she ceases to be a respectable character.

The chief reason for my troubling you with another letter before I receive an answer to the first, is, to intreat the favour of your brother to indulge my wishes that I may choose him for a guardian. Tell him, if he do not accept this trust, he will distress me inexpressibly, for I know no other person on whom I dare rely. His character excites my confidence, and his near relationship to you, my sisterly regard. Procure for me a compliance with this first desire of the heart of your

faithfully affectionate

CLARA WOODFORD.

LETTER XV.

To Miss Woodford.

I AM commissioned, my dear Miss Woodford, by my brother to return an immediate answer to your letter, and to assure you that he esteems the trust you wish to repose in him as an honour conferred upon him; and, as your present situation must be disagreeable

to you, he intends setting out with my sister and me next Monday for Bath, when they will intreat the pleasure of your company back with them, if you can make their place of residence agreeable to you. It would be injurious to you to doubt your acquiescence. Our friendship, which has hitherto subsisted by literary rather than by personal intercourse, will, I hope, be mutually increased by a nearer intimacy.

Mrs. Berkeley intends to resign her house, which is large and commodious, to my brother, and will live in a little hut, as she calls it, adjoining their garden. This place, though small, is convenient and pleasant, and, as Mr. Berkeley comes down at the times of vacation, she thinks it will be more prudent for him to reside with her, than in this family, with two unmarried, young, and not absolutely disagreeable, ladies.

You find I depend on your accepting my brother's and sister's invitation; prepare, my dear, to add to our delights by your society. All this family are as much disposed to love you as your ever affectionate

LUCIA HERBERT.

LETTER XVI.

To Mrs. Berkeley.

Bath, — — — — —

IN parting from you, dearest madam, I felt the insufficiency of temporal pursuits for the enjoyment of perfect happiness. My husband and my sister were with me; the weather, and the journey, promised pleasure; the design of the excursion was the relief of uneasiness, and the increase of our mutual felicity; yet my spirits were exceedingly depressed on bidding you adieu! Most probably, had you accompanied us, some circumstance, now unforeseen, would have allayed our entire satisfaction. Such is the condition of humanity, "this is not our abiding place," yet how many causes have I for thankfulness! I will cease to lament our short separation, and enjoy, whilst I can communicate, pleasure.

We are all safely arrived, and, as I know you are particularly interested for my health, I can assure you I have received benefit as well as amusement from the journey. We have been successful in the principal object of our wishes. Mrs. Selden has, though unwillingly, resigned her trust, and Miss Woodford has, in due form, chosen Mr. Herbert for her guardian.

What could the poor aunt expect from an engagement contracted so late in life, and with a man, the obvious motive of whose attachment, was her fortune? How melancholy a proof is she of the weakness of human nature, which knows not how to choose the ingredients of happiness! The lady is, it seems, remarkably whimsical about her health, and though her strict attention to it was awhile suspended by the novelty of a Bath life, and afterwards by the still more pleasing novelty of a love address, yet the more uniform scenes of domestic retirement will recall her gloomy ideas, and the farther encroachment of time naturally increase her infirmities.

Mr. Selden bears a strong resemblance to the picture Miss Woodford drew of him, yet her contempt of his demerits added some colourings beyond the life.

Our amiable ward prepossessed me in her favour on her first appearance. Her person is extremely agreeable, though not regularly beautiful. Her address is polite, yet friendly. Her heart seems to be already attached to us, with the utmost fervour I may say, for she considers us in too exalted a light. She thinks herself to be in a state of obligation to us, and expresses the gratitude she feels in terms, which, were there the merit she supposes, would be due not to the instrument, but to the first cause. But this is frequently the case with lively, generous spirits—their approbations and dislikes are seldom bounded by mediocrity. Every object of their love and friendship is supremely excellent; whoever occasions their dislike, superlatively disagreeable. Miss Woodford rather idolizes than esteems, and wounds by unmerited panegyric.

My sister and she are united in a strict friendship; I wish her to treat us with the same freedom. Mr. Herbert is delighted with her; he had seen her several times, but never before enjoyed much of her conversation. There is something inexpressibly sprightly in her manner, and witty in her repartees. She will be a most agreeable addition to our family, for she has given us reason to hope that she will be a partaker of our happiness.

Ah! my dear madam, I find nothing here to recompense me for the loss of your conversation. My dearest Mr. Herbert is with me, but though ever amiable, ever excellent, he never appears to be so amiable, so estimable, as when employed in a constant succession of benevolent offices, searching to redress injuries, to mediate differences, to be blessed by the orphan and the widow. I shall rejoice to be restored to the country and to you, yet I will not indulge a murmur whilst we are separated by an act of duty.

Last night we were at the Rooms, where there was a splendid appearance. The attention of the gentlemen was divided between our two lovely friends, but my sister had more than an equal share of admiration. She behaved with such unaffected modesty, on the distinctions she received, that I love her more than ever.

Unexpected visitors compel me to lay down my pen. I will soon resume it, but have now only time to subscribe myself,

dearest madam,

>your most dutifully affectionate

>CAROLINE HERBERT.

Mr. Herbert in continuation.

I CANNOT resist the inclination I feel to add a few words in my Caroline's letter to our mutually respected mother, before I comply with her request that I would seal it. She has told you, madam, how well she supported the journey. She has also acquainted you with the admiration our friendly belles excited, but she has not informed you, and perhaps she is ignorant of the effects of her own charms. She was universally allowed, not only to excel her fair companions, but to be the finest woman ever seen at Bath.—The natural dignity of her person is, you know, heightened by the present circumstance, but the benignity of her mind, impressed on her countenance, was the irresistible attraction.

Truly may woman be called "the Almighty's last, best gift!" O, I discover new excellencies in my amiable wife every day: her disposition is truly angelic; she sees, pities, and gently seeks to remove the infirmities of others, she endeavours to render these subservient to her own improvement, for, with the rest of her virtues, she preserves the truest humility.

If the ladies here were acquainted with the perfections of my Caroline, they would not only wish to resemble her in person, but to imitate her virtues.

Once more, madam, be pleased to accept my reiterated thanks for this inestimable present, and do me the justice to believe that

I am

your most affectionate, dutiful,

and grateful,

C. HERBERT.

LETTER XVII.

To Mrs. Berkeley.

ALREADY, my dear madam, I am tired of this place. I cannot think that the happiness of rational beings can consist in dressing, visiting, walking the parade, and streets, and crowding at the Rooms. The churches indeed are open as well as the Rooms, but where ever diversions are eagerly pursued, the mind becomes unsettled, and duties are seldom regularly performed. Strange! unaccountable! that every one should be so fond of life, and yet so many indifferent to the purposes of living. Youth must be allowed indulgence; it is the proper season of gaiety. Should it not be also considered as the season of improvement? The time for the cultivation of every seed of virtue?

With what peculiar advantages have I been blessed! In parents, who were always the kindest, most indulgent of friends; who, by blending delight with instruction, gave me a preference of their conversation to the gayest society; in a brother attached to me by more than the usual ties of fraternal affection; and all those dear relations anxiously solicitous for the improvement of my mind. I fear I do not sufficiently compassionate those frailties in others, from which my education and your examples have secured me.

Assist me, dear madam, in guarding my heart against any lurking vanity; but I cannot long enjoy any place, where constant engagements fatigue the body, enervate the mind, and unfit it for the noblest exercises. I declare I think even a week at Bath, to partake the whole round of diversions, is too long a time for the enjoyment of them, and yet my spirits still bound (if I may use the expression) at the sprightly notes of a dance; I love a concert, and relish a good theatrical performance, but I think their enjoyment depends on the moderation with which they are pursued.

We have agreed to leave Bath the latter end of this week, and after staying about ten days in London shall set out on our return to my dear mother.

I am still more charmed with Miss Woodford; there is such an unaffected frankness in her acknowledgement of faults, into which she is hurried by her vivacity. But I wish her to restrain every shaft of ridicule, which wounds others, and recoils upon herself.

O! madam, how thankful am I for conjugal happiness. When I observe many of the married parties, (for I cannot call them pairs) of this fashionable world, and see the lords of the creation, particularly, ashamed of being thought capable of a constant attachment, sanctified by the laws of God and man; I pity their weakness, and lament their infatuation. Do they not tacitly reproach themselves for their choice? Or do they not publicly declare that their happiness does not arise from each other's society.

What a miserable being should I have been with one of these contemners of connubial felicity! Would you believe it, madam? Some of these deserters from the matrimonial contract, and other gay flutterers, could not be persuaded for a time that Mr. Herbert and I were those unfashionable creatures, Husband and Wife. They concluded we were merely lovers, and when convinced of their mistake, rallied us most unmercifully on our egregious want of taste. Mr. Herbert is required to be gallant, his wife to be less domestic, and more gay:—A husband, a wife, and a sister to be always of a party, is Gothic to the last degree. Miss Woodford, indeed, enlivens the gravity of such a society; but as Mr. Herbert appears in the character of her guardian, it is thought to be too much in the style of a family picture.

Thanks to Heaven! Mr. Herbert is invulnerable to these attacks. He sees, admires, and applauds every external accomplishment; he esteems and venerates every mental excellence, and in such a manner, as proves that his own heart is gratified by the observation. But he can by his praises, exalt some, without depreciating others, and pay the debt due to every estimable quality, and agreeable appearance, without endangering his fidelity. He is not to be influenced by the maxims and examples of that part of the world, who sacrifice duty at the shrine of fashion. His duty is the basis of his happiness. Such, my dear madam, is the husband of my choice, the son of your approbation!

But whilst I blame the illaudable customs of the inconsiderate, I rejoice in the number of the worthy. How many of both sexes do we know whose minds are an ornament to human nature! yet I must add, that many have not sufficient fortitude to stem the torrent of profane and indecent mirth. Too fearful of incurring public ridicule, they conceal sentiments which do honour to their own hearts, and lest they should make a breach in politeness, really break down a branch of social virtue. They fear to acknowledge a singularity, which is a source of the most delightful consciousness, and would blush at the confession of a hope, which is the only support under disappointment.

Most fervently do I wish that a spirit of virtuous emulation could be excited amongst those who now behold Mr. Herbert's accomplishments with envy: and in my own sex a desire of outshining in real excellence only. O that they would consider of what infinite consequence it is, rather to deserve esteem than to attract admiration! That the autumn and winter of life must succeed to the spring and summer: and that they who survive the blooming seasons without having made a provision for the declining, will find added years are only lengthened misery. In you I see that the matronly time may be enjoyed where the youthful hours have been improved! An imitation of your virtues is the highest ambition of

Your ever dutiful and

    affectionate daughter,

       C. HERBERT.

LETTER XVIII.

To Mrs. Berkeley.

I OUGHT, much earlier, my dear madam, to have remembered that it was my *duty* to have thanked you for every proof I have received of your friendship, and to have contributed with my beloved sister to alleviate the sadness her absence naturally excites. The busy scenes in which we have been engaged, occasioned my silence; but this excuse is insufficient to satisfy myself: Will it be accepted by you? I know your goodness; you will readily forgive me, and I shall more severely blame myself for your indulgence.

My brother and sister have informed you they are charmed with my friend Miss Woodford. She *idolizes* them, yet merrily exclaims, "This sister of yours is a mighty good sort of woman, Lucy; but she has more than her share of admiration. I do not like she should be of my party in a gay circle: She has already robbed me of many a follower—perhaps of many a heart. I believe I shall not love her."

The gay coquet is for unlimited conquest. She tells me it is well she has some estimable qualities to counterbalance "a superfluity of naughtiness," for she owns she pants for a host of admirers. She is versed in all the modes of *captivation* (to use her own expression). She is one moment all encouraging sweetness: the next, all distant reserve, according to the different persons on whom she plays off her arts. Her eye penetrates the hearts of all her beholders, and regulates its motions in conformity.

Is it not somewhat surprising, madam, that a friendship should subsist between two persons, one of whom is avowedly ambitious of universal conquest? But this *rapacity* in my friend has taught me *moderation*. I frequently see her so mortified, if one expected victim remains insensible, or escapes from her chains,—though perhaps ten offer at her shrine, so that I congratulate myself on my superiority of mind, and love her perhaps the better, for permitting me to excel in this respect. The sincere attachment of one man of good sense, good nature,—in short, of such a man as my brother, would gratify my highest ambition. However, I think, "take it for all in all," I shall never be happier than I am at present.

Let this little flutterer enjoy her triumphs. The time will come, I tell her, when she will find a conqueror. "Then, perhaps," said she, "some recreant knight may enlist under your banner, and declare himself a captive to become a conqueror."—"I observe," answered I, "you will not permit me to indulge a more improbable *perhaps*, that when you are enslaved for life, some heart never subjected to *your* power, may confess *mine*."

I told you, dear madam, I wished for such a husband as my brother makes.—Miss Woodford says, he is an adorable husband, but rather too grave, and solemn, rather too little a man of this world. She does not consider her own sensibility, if she thinks she could be happy with a modern husband.

I saw an instance yesterday at the Rooms, of one of these beings, who made a very sweet-tempered wife miserable. He had been absent from Bath for a month, and returned unexpectedly. We had prevailed on his lady to accompany us to the Rooms. Mr. Fowler (that is his name) entered about an hour after us. Mrs. Fowler's emotion on his sudden appearance would have been a very high gratification to him, had he been only an admirer; but as he was her husband, he was mortified by it. He addressed himself, with the utmost ease and politeness to all his acquaintance; but "Your servant, Mrs. Fowler, I thought you had been at home," was the kind salutation to his wife, after he had, with the greatest cordiality, enquired after the health of every common acquaintance. "Do not you remember, my dear," said she, "that you left me indisposed?"— "I see you here, child," replied he, "and therefore conclude you are well."— "But," said she, "will you not tell me you are glad to see me here? I am much rejoiced to see *you*."—He hummed a tune, turned round upon his heel, and mixed with the crowd.

Though Miss Woodford most probably would have ridiculed Mrs. Fowler's joyful surprise at the unexpected return of her husband, his indifference shocked her pride, and alarmed her fears. "Good God! Lucy," said she, "is this the treatment I must expect as a wife? Yet this man, I suppose, was a dying lover. Wretches! they are not worth a moment's pain."

My sister, upon whose arm the dejected wife hung, and who is much admired by Mr. Fowler, took the first opportunity of speaking to him. (What advantages, dear madam, are superior merit and fortune, when they procure to their possessors a happy influence over the conduct of others.) "Do you know," said she, "that your pretended indifference has lowered the spirits of your good lady! and I should surely wrong both her and you if I were to suppose that *your wife* was not entitled to the same attentions you pay to *another's*. You must endeavour to regain your credit with me by appearing more unfashionable, and shewing, even before this assembly, a portion of that tenderness which you must feel for the object of your choice." — "I vow, Mrs. Herbert," answered he, "you are very severe upon me, yet I will endeavour to improve by this lecture:

'From lips like those what precepts fail to move?'

"Come, my dear," continued he, turning to his lady, "excuse your converted Bashful Constant. I *am* glad to see you abroad, and if you and these ladies give me leave, will join your party for the evening."

My brother, who had been walking about the room with a friend, now returned to us, and we were all satisfied. Miss Woodford was engaged with an agreeable partner; I employed myself in making observations on the reunited couple, and my brother and sister are never otherwise than happy.

My sister's eyes sparkled with added lustre from the joy she felt in having contributed to Mrs. Fowler's happiness; I saw that Mr. Fowler watched my brother's looks and behaviour to my sister, and was not unsuccessful in his endeavours to imitate them. Indeed my brother and sister are so much esteemed and admired that I think it is in their power to make *even virtue fashionable*. Of what importance it is to be uniformly good! Such persons need not fear any ill-natured retort, when their benevolence influences them to give advice.

Miss Woodford praises my brother for his inimitable tenderness to his wife; but I tell her she considers that part of his conduct as more meritorious than I can allow it to be; for who does not admire my sister? They seem each to be formed for the other.

How happy must Miss Woodford think herself in such a guardian as my brother, and in such a friend as my sister, and equally happy in my relation to both, and in your friendship

is, dear Madam,

Your most affectionate, obliged,

and grateful

LUCIA HERBERT.

LETTER XIX.

To Mrs. Berkeley.

London. — — — —

AFTER a pleasant journey, we are safely arrived, dearest Madam, and all in high spirits. The addition my brother makes to our society, is no small improvement of our happiness. He was so kind as to meet us about ten miles from town, and escorted us hither. He is very much charmed with Miss Woodford's person and conversation, and she, whether from a mere desire of gaining another admirer, or from a real sensibility of his merit, puts forth all her attractions. I should be very happy in such an alliance; for though I think Miss Woodford has rather a *present* passion for admiration, yet she has just sentiments of female delicacy, and so much softness of disposition, that the man who can gain her heart will inevitably guide her conduct. One who could enjoy her chearfulness, and yet restrain it from deviating into levity, who had real good-nature blended with resolution; such an one, I doubt not, would render her perfectly amiable and completely happy.

She pays much greater attention to my brother, than I have observed in her to any of her flatterers. He was of our party last night, and his eyes were seldom directed to any other object than Miss Woodford: her's were very little excursive, and their conversation appeared to be very interesting. My brother has been constantly with us, and is very desirous we should prolong our stay; but I cannot comply with his request. I am not only impatient to see you again, but another reason for my refusal is, that if he has an inclination to be with us, he can accompany us into the country, and by making you a partaker in them, heighten our delights.

I am certain my brother's heart is attached, and I rather think Miss Woodford's is touched; but she is a little enigmatical. I am somewhat at a loss to distinguish her general fondness of admiration, from her particular regard. She asked me this morning, whether I was really determined to leave London so soon as Monday. I mentioned my promise to you. "Miss Herbert," said she, "will not like town so well when you and her brother have left it. Indeed she will have Mr. Berkeley to gallant her about."

I read her fears. My brother had not hinted before her his resolution to attend us.—"Do you wish to stay longer in town, my dear? I dare say Mrs. Fenning will be equally glad of your's as my sister's company. We shall part from you with regret, but you would soon rejoin us, and the thoughts of seeing my dear mother, and making her happy in the society of my brother, who intends going down with us, will be our consolation." She blushed; "You mistake me, dear Mrs. Herbert, London would have lost its principal charm, when you had left it. Permit me to attend you, and I shall leave the gay town with pleasure."

What think you, dearest madam? are not these prognostics of a regard that will in time prevent all future sallies of coquetry?— For all our sakes I hope so; Miss Woodford would then exchange the insatiable rapacity of universal conquest, which exposes to perpetual disappointments, for a mild and gentle influence over a faithful heart, ever attentive to her happiness.

She has told my brother she is glad he is to be of our travelling party. "I want a Damon," said she, "to enliven the solitude of the country. But you have some rural beauty, I suppose, who will engross all your leisure hours.—His answer was not only gallant, but tender. "This was a compliment I extorted," said she, blushing. "Hush!"—(for he was proceeding) "I forbid, absolutely forbid another syllable on the subject."

On Tuesday then we hope to be with you. My sister has been under a necessity of promising to give Mrs. Fenning a month or six weeks of her company. That lady was quite importunate, as she begins to receive ceremonious visits next week, and wants a female companion on this important occasion.

Adieu! dearest, ever honoured madam. I earnestly wish for the time which may restore to the best of mothers her

ever affectionate and dutiful

daughter,

CAROLINE HERBERT.

LETTER XX.

To Miss Herbert.

My dear Friend,

YOU needed not so earnestly have desired me to write, for who that has a lover, does not want a confidant? I intended to have written sooner, but the assiduities of the lover occasioned the delay.

Mr. Berkeley is most enchantingly enamoured. He lives only for me. He is very amiable, very accomplished, and so forth, but he is not so valuable, so estimable a character as your brother. I am not at all surprised at Miss Berkeley's behaviour, "All for love, or the world well lost," when inspired by such an object; but lest there should not be such another being for me, I will venture to fix my choice upon one who claims alliance with him by virtue, as well as family connextions.

Heigh ho! Lucy, the spirit of coquetry is evaporating very fast. I really believe I can be happy with Mr. Berkeley, for he is very clever, very goodnatured, is pleased with my excursive humours, (N.B. if I marry, I must put some curb on them, lest they should run away with his love) and can improve me by his sententious observations.

But why do I mention marriage? I, who have harangued so much upon the blessings of liberty. Shall I ever submit to be fettered by indissoluble chains? What a change must I experience! I have very little taste for domestic employments. What would the good man say to me, if, when he expected his dinner, I should only give him a taste——— of my forgetfulness. Would he not lose all relish for a vivacity which he might (and not very improperly perhaps) term, giddiness? Ah! Lucy, after all, the single state is best for me. But then

"Who can bear the dread effects of time;
"The pang of despised love, th' opprobrious taunt,
"The insolence of pity; female contumely;

The Wife; or, Caroline Herbert

"When she herself might chance to rule for life
"By one concession?"

Alas! whether as wife, or spinster, that the reign of beauty must soon be at an end, general observation verifies. Shall I then flutter about and command for a few years longer, or shall I now give up the sceptre, take the distaff, and learn to obey?

This man teizes me to make him happy. Ah! I am afraid he will not find it to be in my power. I should be terrified to death if I were ever to be in Mrs. Herbert's present situation. Whimsical enough to fatigue a whole family! and then, to have half a dozen brats perhaps roaring and shrieking about one.—What a scene of confusion! "Chaos would come again." A crazy mother, and noisy infants! Who could bear to come near us? A duet with my spouse, would make little harmony for me I doubt, and a chorus of brats, discord insupportable!—Well then! shall I act my part in life sola, or shall I choose a mate, and enter upon my noviciate of improvement? I doubt I must have a long probation. Here I must pause.

* * * * *

To resume. If I could but contrive, like Mrs. Herbert, to extend my sovereignty, after vowing subjection, I think I could resign the liberty of flying upon the wing of pleasure in pursuit of universal admiration: for to be frank and ingenuous, it is rather an anxious state to be always on the flutter for superiority of beauty. If the envy of the one sex, and the admiration of the other, gratify my vanity, yet the dread of being less envied, by being less admired, destroys my enjoyment.

* * * * *

There is something strangely propitious to love in solitude. Here this man caught me alone in an arbour, and breathed forth such fervent professions that he melted my heart,—and I absolutely owned—a little kind of susceptibility in his favour. Bless me! how he was transported. Simpletons these men! with all their boasted wisdom, to

47

let us see how much we have them in our power; they shew a good opinion of us in thinking we shall not abuse it, but it is a violent, and sometimes an irresistible temptation.

He then began truly to talk of fixing a time for his happiness; but this was too much. I stopt him, told him the subject should have a review another time, but that I had made sufficient concessions for the present. He intreated, but I was peremptory. Is he not my captive! And shall he presume to dictate laws to his conqueror?—He submitted with a sigh.—Poor heart! I wish it has not more cause to despair when it expects to be most gratified.—We left the grove, and Mrs. Herbert meeting us, the scene of courtship entirely closed.

Well, my dear, one comfort is, no change of condition can yet take place. Mrs. Herbert must become a mother before your Clara can think of being a wife. In two months the former expects to commence that character. What will be the season for my transformation I cannot tell, but I assure you it shall be several months before I change the name of

CLARA WOODFORD.

LETTER XXI.

To Miss Woodford.

My dear Clara,

I AM quite fatigued with dress, ceremony, and crowds.—I pine for the country, and hope another week will restore me to it. A month is surely a sufficient sacrifice to form and fashion: but before I mention a word more on this subject let me enter on one more pleasing.

I congratulate you, my friend, on the conquest of a truly valuable heart. Indeed I told you it was secured in your possession before you left town; but you, judging of others by yourself, or perhaps actuated by your usual humility, would not believe Mr. Berkeley was in love. Did you imagine that he too was a trifler? Or, did you affect humility that we might search more attentively for proofs to gratify your vanity.

Believe me, Mr. Berkeley will imitate the bright example my brother sets him; and I hope you will give him a counterpart of my amiable, my excellent sister. At present, be not displeased if I insinuate, that you are not sufficiently sensible of your good fortune. Could it admit a doubt whether it be more eligible to choose a husband with whom you may interchange friendship and confidence, or still to practise the dangerous art of entangling by your charms, even those whom you could not reward with your esteem? The preference, you now seem inclined to give, will increase your own value. No unnecessary delays, I conjure you. As soon as my sister's recovery be perfected (and for all our sakes may heaven preserve her!) I shall expect to be principal bride-maid at your nuptials. As for the subsequent parade, it is, I confess, very fatiguing, but, with your choice, it would be easily supportable.

Mrs. Fenning enjoys the flutter of company. She has been trained for the gay world, while I, a poor rustic, am dispirited, tired, and disgusted, with endless engagements. What shall I be then after a third display? I assure you I was fatigued with the formality, after my sister's appearance, though it was in the country; and I could not refrain from asking her how she could reconcile herself to such an abuse of time; she, whose every hour was before rationally employed.

"We owe to the world," answered she, "a conformity to the customs it has established, where that conformity is consistent with the duties of life. You say, my dear, these visits are merely ceremonious, and sometimes scarcely so innocent, for that they are frequently made only to gratify ill-natured observations. I doubt we must attribute less to friendship than to fashion and curiosity; but it must be our own faults surely if we do not make friends of our observers. Some intercourse with the polite world is requisite to preserve those accomplishments which add a grace to virtue, and recommend the practice of it. Singularity in trifles shows more of affectation than of real superiority."

These were the excellent sentiments of my admirable sister; but Mrs. Fenning considers dress and visits as the principal purposes of life, and her outside is embellished, whilst her mind has remained uncultivated. She is tired to death if we pass an evening by ourselves. She yawns over a book, detests work, and is very much the fine lady. She admires my sister, but she does not endeavour to imitate her. I believe, however, there is more of fashion than relish in her dissipation; and I really think the fault lies rather in her head than heart. She is friendly, though fashionable.

If you can spare time to write me another letter, you will very much oblige

your sincerely affectionate

LUCIA HERBERT.

LETTER XXII.

To Miss Herbert.

THESE people, Lucy, will absolutely annihilate my coquetry; and you, let me tell you, are a party in the same scheme. No constraint I must confess, but a generous reference to my own inclinations, in a point most essential to my happiness, is the only argument urged here. I consulted Mrs. Herbert.

"My dear," said she, "I thank you for this confidence. My brother's and your happiness are equally the subject of my wishes. You are the best judge by what means to obtain it; consult your own heart, and be directed by it. Your prudence will suggest to you," she added, "that coquetry, which is not defensible in a maiden, is still more inexcusable in a wife. My brother is truly good, but to make you happy, you must think him, not only estimable, but agreeable."

Mr. Herbert, when I asked his advice, only said, that as my guardian, and Mr. Berkeley's brother, he was deeply interested in an event, which seemed to promise happiness to both, but that he left the determination to my judgment, and sensibility of Mr. Berkeley's merit.

Then comes your letter, which extols this man, and celebrates my good fortune in high strains. The creature, to be sure, is not despicable, and he addresses me with a pleasing pathos enough. If he can but contrive to make such a husband as your brother, I must be happy.

Last night Mrs. Herbert was indisposed. She had fatigued herself by a long walk on some benevolent visits, and on her return, the heat of the room, and her weariness, occasioned her fainting two or three times. Never was any man so tenderly alarmed as your brother. His whole soul was agitated. He held her reclining head upon his breast, and his cheeks were scarce less pale than her's.

As she revived, he became more composed, and her perfect recovery inspired him with such joy, as shewed evidently that the lover was not extinguished in the husband.

He watches her every look, and I tell him he is impertinent in his frequent inquiries about her health. Yet, Lucy, we should all be pleased with the sedulity which we affect to ridicule. I have desired Mr. Berkeley to be very attentive in observing his brother's every action, that I may have a copy of his perfections, a fair copy, without blot, or omission of one single excellence.

* * * * *

Would you believe it, my dear? This man is not the implicit admirer I thought and wished him to be. Truly he has been finding fault with the manner in which I wear my hair. I looked at him with astonishment.—"You are the first lover, Mr. Berkeley," said I, "who ever presumed to dictate laws to his mistress, and in dress too! You infringe upon the female prerogative, for is not woman sole arbitress of the fashion?"

"You do not, in your heart, blame me, my dear Miss Woodford," said he, "for this instance of my frankness and sincerity. You are superior to those arts by which many ladies wish to enslave the reason of their admirers.—You allow me the exercise of mine; and it is from this exercise of my rational faculties, that you owe your influence over my heart."—"Ah! flatterer, you celebrate me for being faultless, that you may have the pleasure of expatiating on my follies."—"No, Miss Woodford, I do not attribute perfection to any mortal; but I think you so emulous of it, that you are not afraid of hearing truth; and as for your sex being the arbitress of the mode, give me leave to tell the amiable arbitress of my fate, that the desire of pleasing our's is your actuating principle. If you direct the mode, we influence you."

"O, wretch! what a thought!—Though I dare answer for it, if there were not a man in the world, we should sit all day in our nightcaps." (aside to Mrs. Herbert). She betrayed my secret, so I made my exit, for the two he-creatures exulted beyond endurance.

* * * * *

Now, Lucy, what do you think of this being to whom I have not yet given authority to address any thing to me but flattery? Does he not lord it well? I shall be as very a wife as obedience can render me, if I now resign the reins of despotic sway.—No, it must not be—his every idea of me should include perfection. Yet, to be serious, I like him not the worse for his freedom; but as to altering my manner of dress, not one atom must bend in subjection, for that would be giving up every thing. Perhaps when he is quite reconciled to this fashion, I may abate somewhat in the excess of it.

* * * * *

I am retired, my dear, from a scene of humiliation. A Mrs. Wright drank tea with us this afternoon, and brought with her a Miss Elden—really a prettyish woman. I will confess too that she was elegantly dressed, and not in the extremity of the fashion. She is modest and reserved, and entirely free from pride and affectation. So much justice demands—now piqued vanity takes its turn.

Mr. Berkeley praises this Miss Elden more than becomes the lover of another woman: that woman present too: shameful! I am not accustomed to hear another commended at my expense. Is it not mortifying to have another elevated on my ruins? Here my poor dress has been taken to pieces, and Miss Elden's is set up as the standard of the proper and becoming. I am piqued, as I said before, but you too much resemble your sister to pity me.—Mr. Herbert thinks her very pleasing! "She dresses like my Caroline," was his expressive observation. Such a loving husband! Nothing charms him but as it agrees with that idea of female excellence, which he takes from Mrs. Herbert. I am pettish and displeased.

* * * * *

I take up my pen in a different humour. Resentment has subsided, and the tenderest commiseration has taken place. Mrs. Herbert is very ill. Mr. Herbert is very anxious, and very miserable. Mrs. Berkeley and Mr. Berkeley are deeply agitated, and your Clara is shocked and terrified.—Lord bless me! how should I support such a state? I, who have not the mental resources Mrs. Herbert has. Adieu! till to-morrow.

* * * * *

Mrs. Herbert is better. She has had a fine night, and is as cheerful as ever, to the great delight of all her friends, and to the inexpressible joy of her husband.

She desires me to tell you she shall be very glad if you do not exceed the time mentioned in your last letter; unless some projected amusement solicits your stay, and she then begs you to prolong it: but for my part I entreat that you would be with us as soon as possible, or I shall be absolutely deserted. The sick-room will confine Mrs. Berkeley almost as closely as her daughter. I shall be tired of keeping chamber, and yet must in decency be more there than with the gentlemen.—Come then, and relieve the anticipated distresses of

your faithful and affectionate,

CLARA WOODFORD.

LETTER XXIII.

To Mrs. Bennett.

YOU remember, my dear madam, it was agreed between us, that we might continue to be sincere friends without becoming constant correspondents. I know you hate writing, and I am not fond of it, but upon great occasions.

The birth of a young Herbert deserves to be celebrated by my pen— Mrs. Herbert became a mother last Wednesday, and in the antediluvian phrase, "is as well as can be expected." The boy is a jolly boy, has fine strong lungs, and makes more different faces in a moment, than ever coquet practised before her glass.

Mrs. Herbert has begun to perform the maternal office. What a horrid scene of confinement opens, from the care of this little squaller! But she is quite domesticated. I believe the dear good matron has scarcely a thought which does not centre in husband, child, or mother. What a trio! You, my good Coz., are not much more of a modern, only your duties are not enlarged to the sphere of brat-rearing. Never repine, child! 'tis a circumstance which rather demands your gratitude.

Miss Herbert and I have a dull time of it. I should say I have, for she, poor imitative being, is commenced downright aunt in thought, word, and deed. Truly she must nurse sometimes, though I tell her she will give her sister a feveret by the fright which her awkwardness occasions.

I dare not attempt to handle the little creature, lest I should let it fall, or indulge Lucy with an opportunity of retaliating. Besides, if it should attack our ears with a squall while in my arms, or even make a wry face, the mother would stain my fostering character with the imputation of causing it.

The Wife; or, Caroline Herbert

Mr. Herbert is all rapture. He passes the greatest part of the day in the sick chamber; and how do you think he employs himself? He must play at lullaby too. The little animal is laid on his lap upon a pillow, and he prates to it like any experienced nurse. At other times he reads to the poor prisoner, who, though I think she must be heartily tired of her confinement, is all thankfulness and serenity.

What a uniform succession of events! To drink caudle, see her child drest, and to feed it; to hear the harangue of an old whining crone, who pours forth the antiquated expletives of praise over the little reptile, who lies sprawling on her lap: these are the joys of a lying-in woman! are they not captivating?

Yet I own Mrs. Herbert has a most rational enjoyment, which throws a cheering light even over these scenes of still life. What a husband has she to be thankful for!

As to Mrs. Berkeley she is delighted with the infantile scenes, and to be the principal. She will spoil the boy; I can see she will; but they laugh at my remarks, and I ridicule their folly. Mr. Berkeley professes fondness for his nephew. Such a little machine to set to work the minds of rational people!

* * * * *

I really believe, Mrs. Bennett, I could in time love this little being. I was alone in Mrs. Herbert's chamber about an hour since. She was asleep; the nurse below, enjoying the perpetual motion of her own tongue, when lo! the babe set up a most outrageous cry.—I was alarmed; quite upon the flutter. What now is to be done? I'll e'en take him up. Accordingly, recollecting the manner and form in which these feeble mortals are to be touched, I compassed the mighty deed, fed him, quieted him, and then, charmed with his good humour, I contemplated his placid features, till I actually gave him a kiss.

He is a very pretty child. I do love him; and I considered what claim such helpless innocents have to our care and attention. Who knows but I may one day be a fond mother. I won't answer for it, however, nor do I desire the trial.—But to return.

While I was sitting with little Charles's hand in mine, the door softly opened, and Mrs. Berkeley with Mr. Herbert entered. I was ashamed of my office, (having protested against it) till I saw I gave real pleasure to the grandmother and father. The latter told me he had a higher regard for me than ever.

Mrs. Herbert now awaked, and joined her thanks for my attention to her little one. She pressed my hand, and told me she hoped for an opportunity of repaying me for this most endearing proof of love. I assure you I intend to nurse every day; but perhaps 'tis only the novelty of the employment that pleases me. I think, however, I must love this infant for its parents' sakes.

This is hitherto entirely a nursery *letter*, but I have a trifling subject to mention for a little variety. I know Miss Herbert informed you when you were in town of Mr. Berkeley's attachment to me. I have only time to add, that I believe I shall like him well enough to make him an husband. Can you have any idea that he will have a good wife in

your ever affectionate,

CLARA WOODFORD

LETTER XXIV.

To Mrs. Bennett.

ANOTHER great occasion demands my pen. I may possibly lose the half of my fortune. You know my aunt's jointure on her decease reverts to me. Mrs. Selden, however, intends to withhold it, and insists that by my uncle's will she has a power of disposing of every thing.

My guardian, foreseeing some trouble from this knavish proceeding, determined on a journey to town. My aunt declares, (and her will, she says, shall confirm it) that the jointure was only to be mine in case my behaviour pleased her; otherwise she had the sole disposal of it.

Luckily, (providentially, Mrs. Herbert would say,) my uncle had not only informed me how the matter was circumstanced, but he had given me an exact copy of the will he put into her hands. They have certainly forged a will for my uncle.

I have also in my possession the letters which passed between my father and Counsellor Wilson; and after my father's death, those between my uncle and that gentleman on this subject; which mention the cutting off the entail on my brother's decease, and securing the estate to me. My aunt was ignorant of this trust, and on this ignorance the forgery was planned.

My presence was necessary, and, as the time of Mr. Herbert's continuance in town on this account, is uncertain, Mrs. Herbert, who is perfectly recovered, resolved to accompany us. Little Charles must of consequence be of our party. Mr. Herbert will most probably stay the remainder of the winter. So here we all are, except Mrs. Berkeley, whose health is always injured by the town air.

Mr. Herbert determines to endeavour to bring Mr. Selden to reason, without the disagreeable resources of the law. I hope he will have no great trouble, yet I sometimes fear the worst. How much am I indebted to my guardian! He immediately gave up every thing but what related to my affairs. Excellent man!

Mr. Berkeley came to town with us. His behaviour on this threatened diminution of my fortune, shews the sincerity of his affection; but matrimony is now the least subject of my thoughts. I protest I sometimes wish this man had made choice of Miss Herbert.—She would have suited him much better than I ever shall. I wonder he never liked her, for she is a very amiable girl. He says indeed that he always considered her as a second sister: it was a foolish fancy to entertain a fraternal affection, when he might have secured his happiness with the same person by a conjugal attachment.

Farewell, dear Mrs. Bennett. My spirits are not quite so much elevated as usual, but my heart is always equally, and very

affectionately your's,

CLARA WOODFORD.

LETTER XXV.

To Mrs. Berkeley.

Dearest and honoured Madam,

THE sudden and unexpected summons which occasioned our separation affected me very sensibly, but circumstances proved its necessity, and Mr. Herbert's guardianship to Miss Woodford required it as a duty. I fancy our stay will not be very short. You know Mr. Herbert loves company, and enjoys, within the bounds of moderation, the town and its diversions. He has confined himself on my account for many months. He shall not be influenced to return sooner than his own inclination prompts him.

My dear little charge bore his journey beyond expectation. The delightful employ of nursing him will prevent me from being much in company, and from partaking many diversions; but Mr. Herbert can escort my sister and Miss Woodford. I am not surprised that he has a taste for company, as he possesses every requisite which can render conversation delightful and instructive.

You are as well acquainted with the merits of this excellent man as myself, but where the heart is attached, it will naturally dilate on the qualities of its beloved object; and yet how weak is the force of words, when they should express the tenderest emotions of the soul!

Mr. Herbert, in the midst of a gay world, is neither dissipated by pleasure, nor engrossed by business. He has been several times at Mr. Selden's, but that gentleman does not choose to be visible. Mr. Herbert is unwilling to blast the character of Mr. Selden, and desirous of shewing him he has a power of demanding the estate the other withholds.—My sweet boy calls loudly for me. Adieu! dearest madam.

* * * * *

The Wife; or, Caroline Herbert

The dear infant is sunk to sleep in my lap. I will endeavour to scribble another line, and if I borrow a few moments to give him a look or a kiss, his fond grandmother shall repay herself by taking upon her the office of nurse; a province the mother now seldom suffers to be invaded.

Indeed I often jest with Miss Woodford on the vicissitudes in her inclination. "Novelty, my dear Mrs. Herbert," she says, "is a powerful charm for light minds.—The matter had nothing else to recommend it.—Yes, upon second thoughts, I believe I congratulated myself on my own expertness in handling the brat. I have shewn my abilities, and am satisfied with applause. I love you mighty well, Charles! but no more nursing, do you hear, my boy? It destroys the whole system of fashionable regulations. I shall be a poor unsteady wife, Mrs. Herbert.—Warn your brother."

My sister is constant in her attendance on the sweet babe. She is really a fourth parent to him.

Miss Woodford, I believe, is very much engrossed by this threatened diminution of her fortune; and yet Mr. Herbert tells her he thinks it is in no danger, and she disclaims being at all affected by the affair; but her liveliness is so frequently interrupted, she is so often lost in meditation, that either this law matter, or the thought of approaching matrimony disturbs her mind.

She spoke much less than usual during the journey; indeed I have observed for some time past that she has had intervals of gravity, but her natural vivacity has never been so much clouded as now.

To contract so solemn an engagement as marriage, where new cares and duties alarm us with fears of being oppressed with the one, and unequal to the discharge of the other, is it not sufficient to cast a gloom over the brightest prospects?

"What a change!" she often says; "I, whose employments have all centered in dress and pleasure, must then begin to think of prudence and oeconomy. I, who have had only to consult my glass, must, when I marry, learn to consult—my husband."

My brother is particularly urgent with her now to fix his happy day, but she will hear nothing of it at present. "What! marry a law suit? a contested estate? Imprudent Mr. Berkeley!"

Miss Woodford looked into my room just now: "You are complaining of me, Mrs. Herbert, or else it is my own guilty conscience that makes me suspicious.—My mother-elect has not the highest opinion of her intended daughter-in-law. I fear she will have a worse, for positively I can never make the wife I ought to be to Mr. Berkeley."—"If you prefer any other, my dear"—"No, madam, but he is too good for me. However I'll try to improve.—Six months may cause a total revolution in my sentiments. But finish your letter, and then I'll take your pen."

I will conclude with an assurance, which, though unnecessary, I know is always pleasing, that

I am,

dear and honoured madam,

your dutiful, affectionate, and

ever grateful daughter,

C. HERBERT.

Miss Woodford in continuation.

MRS. Herbert, madam, is so excellent that I despair of ever equalling, and am therefore almost discouraged from an attempt at imitating her.—I know not what magical influence may be produced by an alliance with her, but in the common series of cause and effect, I shall never be worthy of claiming a nearer affinity with her, nor, though I can avow a tender and reverential regard for you, shall I ever, I fear, be deserving the additional title of daughter to that of

your most obliged and

sincerely affectionate

CLARA WOODFORD.

LETTER XXVI.

To Mrs. Bennet.

AFTER more than a month's daily attendance on Mr. Selden, my guardian has at last seen him, and forced an audience.

He was going out of his own house as Mr. Herbert came up to the door. His confusion betrayed his guilt. I shall not attempt to send particulars of their conversation. The important result was, that Mr. Selden told Mr. Herbert, his wife only wished to reduce Miss Woodford to a sense of her duty, by threatening her with a loss of that reversion, of which they knew they could not, nor ever intended to deprive her. They parted friends, and I hope there is an end of this matter.

I think we are not quite so happy as we were, and yet I scarcely know the reason. The day after I sent my last letter to you, we were invited to be of the party with Sir Robert and Lady Millbank, at a route and private dance. Mrs. Herbert could not conveniently accompany us, but, as she insisted that Mr. Herbert, Lucy, and I, should not confine ourselves on her account, we agreed to accept the invitation.

Mr. Berkeley had engaged me for a partner. Mr. Herbert sat down to cards, and Miss Herbert danced with a young nobleman, a Lord Wilton, a handsome, genteel, and, to all appearance, accomplished man, who was of the same college with Mr. Herbert. He is very gay, and though he chose Miss Herbert for a partner (perhaps because I was engaged; no vanity at all in the supposition) yet he divided his devoirs very equally between us.

I believe Mr. Berkeley was not in a state of felicity, but I could not help shewing that I was very happy. Birth, fortune, dress, and genteel manners were strong recommendations in Lord Wilton's favour; and to say the truth, I rather wished to have exchanged partners with Miss Herbert; not that I was influenced by partiality for the man, but his station:—There is an irresistible charm in rank and title.

Between his intervals of attention to us, he attached himself to Mr. Herbert with remarkable assiduity. The merits of this amiable man disarm even envy itself. To know him is a defence for a woman against any ill-passion. No one, who knows and does not endeavour to imitate him, can be worthy of a serious thought.

Lord Wilton waited on us next day, and, to our mortification, (your pardon, Lucy) seemed to gaze with more admiration on the matron, than on the spinsters; but he soon put us in good humour again by the volubility of his compliments, and we were all pleased with his conversation.

Mr. Herbert has returned his visit, and found a large and brilliant company. Lord Wilton has a sister, who is married to Lord D——, and he intreated Mrs. Herbert would permit him to introduce Lady D—— to her as a visitor. Accordingly she came a few days since with the two lords. She is a handsome and very lively woman. By frequenting the circles of the great, and being accustomed to shine in them, she has laid aside the blush of modesty, and ridicules silent diffidence.

A party was proposed for the play. Mr. Herbert declined going, unless Mrs. Herbert could accompany him. Lady D—— laughed at the *droll* refusal, as she called it: "Are you always dangling at your wife's apron string?" said she, "Or do you make the pap, or undress the child? Your lady, perhaps, from the horrid office she has undertaken, may be unable to go, but she is too reasonable to immure you in a nursery. Besides, sir, do you think Mrs. Herbert can have no companion when you and these ladies leave her? I am sure she need never be at a loss for society."

Her raillery however had no effect; he gazed tenderly on Mrs. Herbert to read her inclination in her looks: her desire of obliging him preponderated over every other, and she agreed to be of the party.

We went, and had a very agreeable evening. Lady D——
endeavoured to make Mr. Herbert quite gallant, and he was really
more lively and agreeable than I ever before saw him. You know
both he and Mrs. Herbert have naturally a thoughtful turn, yet he
loves company. The still domestic life has the most charms for
her, yet I must add that she gives up her own, whenever she can
gratify his inclination.

But how I wander! I was not much pleased with Lord Wilton; the
man seems to have no eyes but for Mrs. Herbert, and his tongue is
officious in her praise.

As we past Lord D——'s in returning from the play, they
intreated we would step in for half an hour. Lady D—— told Mr.
Herbert his child would certainly be asleep, and therefore he
could not take nurse's office that night. Mr. Herbert however
would not assent. He knew Mrs. Herbert did not wish to comply
with the request. I always love to prolong a frolic, but it could not
be.—With what delight did this excellent man return with his
Caroline! She thanked him in the tenderest manner for his
goodness.

We returned Lady D——'s visit last week. She was very
importunate with us to stay supper. Mrs. Herbert declined the
invitation as her young charge was not quite well. I was disposed
to stay. Lord Wilton was peremptory for Mr. Herbert's making
one at the card-table.

Lady D—— resumed her raillery on Mr. Herbert. After supper
she proposed toasts, and told him, as he could think of no other
woman, he should be permitted to give *his wife*. He turned off the
laugh, gave a very agreeable lady, and told Lady D—— that,
though his heart was attached only to one, his good wishes, and a
just sense of their merit, extended to all the fair sex. He added,
that the excellent qualities of his wife served as a criterion by
which to judge of others. Lady D—— did not relish his answer.

I cannot help observing, my dear Mrs. Bennet, that a strong shield of resolution is necessary to repel the darts of ridicule, which are levelled at the fidelity of the matrimonial life! and yet without faithful love how dreadful must be the engagement! Do not they render themselves completely despicable, who contemn and make a jest of plighted vows?

I am angry with Lady D— — for her ill-judged mirth. Mr. Herbert is not the proper object of light reflections. Such a man ought to be in love to complete his character. His tenderness is rational and manly. His heart feels more than he wishes to express before others, yet his eyes betray his invariable attachment. Happy the woman who preserves such a lover in a husband!

Mr. Berkeley, I am told, will make me as happy if it be not my own fault. Perhaps he would, but I am not able to answer for myself, therefore I will make him no promises.—He is not easy I doubt, but would he be more so if I was to become his wife? Ah! no, he does not know me. Our hearts are not allied, I fear, as those ought to be who contract the most solemn engagement in the sight of Heaven.—I do not know what to do with him—perhaps I may make him a husband. That may be the next revolution. At present my thoughts are more than a little confused.

I told you we were not quite happy. Since our visit we have heard many things to the disadvantage of Lord Wilton's character. Mr. Herbert does not seem to discredit them, and yet he continues the acquaintance. He approves, however, Mrs. Herbert's proposal of declining any farther intercourse with Lady D— —, but Lord Wilton has, I doubt, too much influence over him. He is from home more than usual, and when with us is thoughtful, and sometimes even melancholy.

Yet the same, if not a greater degree of tender regard is paid to Mrs. Herbert, whose eyes and looks shew her mind is not quite at ease. Perhaps he has been rallied for his domestic enjoyments. Ah! is it possible we should ever be ashamed of our happiness!—Miss

Herbert is displeased, Mr. Berkeley dissatisfied, and we are all of us, I believe, discontented.

* * * * *

I have your's, and enjoy the hopes of soon seeing you in town; but surely you will stay longer than a fortnight. Resolve to become a woman of the world, and bring your husband to civilize him a little; for at present he is quite a rustic. What should keep you at home? You have no squallers, the horses can plough without you, the earth will bring forth its increase; and I would not have you return till it has put on its brightest livery.—Adieu, my dear. — Believe me to be your

      sincerely affectionate

      CLARA WOODFORD.

LETTER XXVII.

To Charles Herbert, Esq.

WHAT ails you, Herbert? What was the occasion of your precipitate retreat from company last night? Engaged for the evening, surrounded by a most agreeable party—music, dancing, every circumstance conspiring to exhilarate the spirits, and expand the heart! how could you, with the apathy of a Stoic, break from the engagement, and quit such society?

I saw you go out of the room, but I had no idea that you meant not to return.—The ladies suppose that your wife had fixed your time, and that you were afraid of transgressing.—If so, poor Herbert!—then you are fallen indeed!

Tell me the reason, the cause rather. I am, on the tiptoe of expectation,

your's,

WILTON.

LETTER XXVIII.

To Lord Wilton.

YOU are dissatisfied with my retreat, my Lord, and I fear you will despise my apology.—I was apprehensive of trusting myself any longer in the dangerous company to which you introduced me.—I saw through the character of the ladies whom you described as women of honour, of spirit, of fire, disposed to communicate pleasure, and enjoy life. My vanity was gratified, my senses were ensnared, but my heart and my reason revolted against the tendency of my feelings. I thought on my Caroline, on her virgin charms, on her conjugal attachment, on her unsullied purity, and the recollection raised a blush on my cheek.—I resolved to avoid temptation, and precipitately withdrew.

If, my Lord, you feel for me the friendship you profess, you will not excuse, but commend me.—The noblest office of friendship, is to invigorate the performance of duty. Be your's such, my Lord!—Such is the regard I feel for you. I will endeavour to break the ties of every dangerous connection, but shall ever be

your Lordship's sincere friend.

CHARLES HERBERT.

LETTER XXIX.

To Miss Herbert.

O MY dear Miss Herbert, reports have reached this place, in regard to your brother.—Surely they cannot be true!—My child cannot be less dear to the man who seemed to live only for her;—yet a mother's fears are ever awake. Perhaps I unnecessarily torment myself.—From you, my dear, I request an immediate explanation.— My son, though free from that rashness of disposition, which often precipitates into vice, and though he loves Mr. Herbert, not only as a brother, but as a friend, is not a proper person to be consulted on this occasion.—I dare not solicit my daughter to remove my doubts.— Her principles will not permit her to accuse a husband even to a tender parent.

When I parted from my Caroline, I requested that she would write to me every week, and that she would communicate to me every circumstance that happened.—A request, which appeared to be unnecessary to so dutiful and affectionate a child, but which was dictated by the fondness of a tender parent.—She promised, and for some time complied with that promise.—Indeed she has never failed to write;* but her letters are short. They contain nothing to relieve, nor perhaps to realize my fears.

I intreat you, Miss Herbert, to answer me sincerely, or, notwithstanding the inconvenience my health has always suffered in London, I will undertake the journey.—Whatever be the result of my enquiry, I shall be easier than under this cruel suspense.

I am, my dear,

your affectionate

ELIZABETH BERKELEY.

LETTER XXX.

To Mrs. Berkeley.

WOULD to Heaven, my dear madam, it was in my power to remove your uneasiness!—As you earnestly desire an answer, and your presence here would only add to distress, I must unwillingly confirm the disagreeable reports with which you have been afflicted.—Yet perhaps my brother is more deceived than criminal.

Never did any man appear more truly excellent till within the last few months.—Never did any man feel more strongly the influence of love and esteem.—Never was any woman more deserving than my sister of both.—He cannot cease to love and esteem her, nor be lost to the principles with which his mind was early imbued; yet I am afraid these sentiments have not been able to preserve him from the infection of bad example.

He has renewed an intimacy with a Lord Wilton—a wretch, whose specious appearance must have deceived my brother into an opinion that he is worthy of his friendship.—His unsuspecting confidence will be an endless source of remorse to him, and occasion lasting uneasiness to his friends. How far it has betrayed him I know not, but Mr. Berkeley's and my remonstrances have been hitherto ineffectual to break off the acquaintance.

My sister's charms, I really believe, have captivated this vile Wilton's heart. His attentions have been distressing to her. Her unaffected indifference to all his fine speeches, her unremitted sedulity to please my brother, (yet these sedulities, "not obvious, not obtrusive,") convinced his Lordship, I suppose, of the folly of his attempts.— Probably he revenges himself on her cruelty by withdrawing her husband, or perhaps he flatters himself that my brother's deviations will in time warp her from duty.—But her conduct is so nobly uniform, it must destroy every presumptuous hope.—Dear creature! she pines in secret, and endeavours to assume an appearance of chearfulness, whilst her looks convey a faithful representation of her mind.

Notwithstanding our friendship, she has never uttered a reproachful word of my brother. Even to you I find she has not disclosed her uneasiness. I admire, I reverence those virtues which I should be incapable of practising. My temper, naturally impetuous, would, on such an occasion, have hurried me into excesses my reason would have condemned, and which might have produced fatal effects.

I own I have upbraided my brother—perhaps too severely—at least my sister's tenderness would certainly deem all expostulation to be severity.—But I cannot bear such excellence should suffer; yet let me not, madam, add to your affliction, but permit me to open a prospect of relief.—Rely on the goodness of my brother's heart, and his love for your Caroline. A false shame may deter him from a confession of his fault:—my reproaches may have irritated, instead of convincing him: I will not think he dare indulge an idea that my sister knew I meant to arraign his conduct.—He must be more sensible of her virtues than to entertain such a suspicion.—Had I imitated her example, his reformation might have been sooner effected. I condemn my hasty, impertinent zeal. I will endeavour to gain my sister's confidence. I will, like her, attempt to reclaim by sweetness. Mr. Berkeley's influence may be still successful. You shall soon receive another letter from me, and I will write to you constantly.— Let me beg, dear madam, you will not mention to the gentle sufferer the information I have given you: but I beg pardon for the suggestion.

Excuse my freedom, and regard only the good intention that actuates

your ever devoted and faithful

LUCIA HERBERT.

LETTER XXXI.

To Mrs. Berkeley.

IT is only to you, dear madam, that I will convey the overflowings of my heart.—When I had finished my letter, I went up to my sister's dressing room. Little Charles lay asleep on her lap; her eyes were intently fixed on him, and the tears stole silently down her cheeks.

I shut the door.—I softly approached her with the reverential awe due to a superior being. She heard not my step, but started at the sound of my voice. I could not restrain my emotions on a scene so affecting; I clasped my arms about her;—a look of self-reproach upbraided my intrusion.

"Ah! my dear sister," cried I, "what is the occasion of these tears? And why are you so unkind as to weep alone?—The penetrating eye of friendship has long observed your uneasiness. Tell me, my beloved Caroline"—

A fine glow overspread her sweet face: she gently put me from her.—"I have nothing to impart, my Lucy," said she; a smile faintly dimpled her cheek; her averted eye betrayed what her words attempted to conceal.

"Now, my sister," replied I, "you wound me by your reserve,—my brother is unkind,—he has lost his relish for virtue. He is unworthy of you.—I pity you from my soul, and I must seek and upbraid him for being the cause of such uneasiness."

I was going, when she hastily pulled me back; "Ah! my Lucy," said she, "how severe you are! Dear, unhappy, mistaken man, he is more to be pitied than condemned.—What must he suffer! O that wretch Lord Wilton! I date the commencement of my misery from the renewal of that acquaintance: yet, my sister, be not precipitate in your conclusions. I think I could answer for him with my life, that he is free from actual guilt. His heart, his esteem are still mine. That his inclinations have wandered, alas! I doubt not. Consider the frailty of human nature; consider the company into which Lord Wilton allures him;—yet Mr. Herbert's principles will, I hope, preserve, or soon restore him."

She wrung her clasped hands. She shed a flood of tears; then raising her fine eyes, she seemed to supplicate for her child the protection of Heaven, while the sweet babe, insensible of her grief, lay smiling upon her lap.

I was unable to answer; and she added, "I know not what I ought to do—but I am determined never to reproach him. Have I ever discovered any tendency to a suspicious temper? I would not have him imagine I am uneasy, lest he should, with too much severity, accuse himself."

I could not forbear exclaiming, "Excellent woman! he is unworthy of such tender solicitude."—"Ah! my dear," answered she, "there are times when human nature is more liable than at others, to be overcome by temptations. And, alas! the manners of the age are dangerous. We have escaped his trials, but we have no reason to conclude, that under similar circumstances, we should have superior strength for conquest. His deviation proves that constant vigilance, unremitted attentions, are requisite to support the best principles."

"Your conduct," answered I, "displays the brightest example to our sex.—I am amazed at your fortitude. I have seen you receive my brother with a face veiled in the sweetest smiles, whilst I am certain your heart bled from a painful sensibility! When he has caressed his little boy with a conscious glow, arising from reflections on his own abasement, your eyes have glistened with hope; yet how studiously have you avoided any particular attention to his behaviour!"

"Do not," said she, blushing, "do not so highly praise a conduct, by which alone I could reasonably expect to regain my husband's affections. Believe me, wandering inclinations will not be recalled by tears or reproaches. These will rather harden or fatigue, for compassion only will not sufficiently re-animate a heart susceptible of softer impressions, and which has in some measure lost its relish for the object which inspired them. He still esteems me; it is only by a conduct supported on Christian principles, I can hope to increase that esteem; and only by the tenderest unobtrusive attentions, I can endeavour, with any prospect of success, to re-kindle his inestimable affection.—Is there not some fault in me to justify this change? I wish him to think me amiable as well as estimable."

"Fault!" interrupted I, "you are the brightest mirror of perfection. I cannot bear you should have any doubts of yourself. He only is blameable, and deserves reproach. Indeed, indeed, you are absolutely faultless."

"You are much too partial," said she; "yet my heart acquits me of a thought injurious to my love or virtue.—But, ah! Lucy, why did you force me to explain the cause of my uneasiness? Had I chosen a confidant, I had not deserved to have found a friend: but to upbraid Mr. Herbert, to reproach him as you suggested.—O, my sister! how could you calmly intend to make him uneasy?"

"For *his* good—for *your* happiness," cried I.—"His misery is the consequence of his degeneracy."—"Do not give so harsh a name," answered she, "to his deviation. Indeed, Lucy, you are too severe; his mind is fraught with every excellence. A pretended friend, dangerous connections, have drawn him aside from the path of duty; but, I hope, he will soon recover it."

She paused, but soon resumed. "Would it be for his good, do you say, mildly to represent to him his danger? I think I can abstract self, and feel only for his present peace and future felicity? I know not how to support the thought that he should degrade himself to a lower degree of eternal happiness.—And O! to think that he may be snatched from the world in the commission of a fault, or whilst harbouring a criminal wish or intention!"

Tears prevented her farther utterance. I could not speak. I threw my arms around her; we mingled our tears. The sound of voices in the next room now interrupted us. My sister only added, pressing my hand, "Remember, my dear Lucy, you extorted from me a secret I never intended to divulge, and preserve it with inviolable caution."

The entrance of the servant to acquaint us that company was below, prevented my answer. We endeavoured to adjust our looks, and went down. Soon after I retired to my chamber to give you this intelligence.

My sister is so dear to me, that I shall not taste of happiness till she enjoys it. May some method occur to you of restoring it, is the most fervent wish of,

dear madam,

your truly sympathising,

LUCIA HERBERT.

LETTER XXXII.

To Miss Herbert.

Her second letter not received.

Dear Miss Herbert,

IT is difficult to determine what situation will most contribute to our ease or happiness. I, who lately imagined suspense to be the most racking state, and hoped relief even from a certainty that my fears were just, am now convinced that painful suspense was less tormenting, than the dreadful explanation which succeeds it.

O, my dear, your letter pierced my soul. Is it possible? Can my child, the darling of my heart, the admiration and delight of all who beheld and conversed with her, can she be neglected by a husband to whom her merit must be most conspicuous? Who owes, perhaps, in a great measure to her those refined sentiments which I once fondly hoped would have invariably influenced his conduct.

How soon, alas! are all my flattering expectations vanished! perhaps I indulged too much the satisfaction of my heart!—perhaps I imagined my dear child placed above the reach of adversity. I thought her virtues secured her from tasting the bitter cup of affliction! Sad conviction of my error.

Forgive the effusions of a mother's despair, who finds the dear support of her life rendered miserable, by the unkindness of him, whose duty it is to protect and reward her virtue! What will become of that sweet babe (whose birth was the subject of our thankfulness, and the completion of our happiness) if his father dissipates fortune, health, and peace?—Short-sighted mortals!

How will my generous son, that tender brother, that affectionate friend, how will he support his sister's misery, his friend's degeneracy? Will not her sufferings awaken in him a resolution to

revenge his wrongs, though on a person lately so dear to him?—
Thought is dreadful—imagination distracts me!

Can you, my dear Miss Herbert, can you pity and excuse the tedious
repetitions my griefs occasion?—My heart overflows—it will dictate
to my pen its wretchedness.—But you will not blame me for
indulging this transitory relief, nor think the expression of my fears
the mere weakness of age.

Do not, my dear Miss Herbert, impart to my child your suspicions of
her husband.—Do not betray her into a confession of unkindness. I
know her so well, that were you to force from her an accusation of
Mr. Herbert, she would despise herself as having been guilty of a
breach of duty.

I am at a loss to know how to act. Suppose I write to him—suppose I
mention the suggestions of the world, and assure him of the
inviolable secrecy his wife has preserved. Shall I represent to him her
wretchedness, made still more deplorable by that reserve which she
thinks it her duty to support?

I will lay down my pen, and consider.

* * * * *

Your second letter, my dear Miss Herbert, was put into my hands,
whilst I was revolving in my mind what conduct I ought to observe,
in respect to your first.—I find I was too late in my cautions.—You
have forced from her the fatal secret.—How I pity her distress! How
I admire the noble conflict!—Tenderness for her unworthy husband
combated with her desire of preserving his character—that character
which he has forfeited?

How does he dare to slight the affection, which confers on him more
honour than all his fancied endowments?—No, I will not write to
him;—I am not calm enough—my daughter's happiness is too dear
to me, to permit me to hazard the entire forfeiture of it; and indeed I

am certain even her existence depends on her hopes of regaining his heart.

Inconsiderate, blind Herbert!—But I am writing to his sister, and, as I cannot forbear to mention him with the resentment of an injured mother, I will add only, on this subject, may God give him grace to repent!—For my dear daughter's sake I wish him repentance, and even for his own,—poor thoughtless man!—though he has destroyed the peace of his once fond mother, and your

ever affectionate Friend,

ELIZABETH BERKELEY.

LETTER XXXIII.

To Charles Herbert, Esq.

IF you can conquer that egregious sheepishness, which makes you dislike the conversation of fine and lovely women, because your wife does not relish, nor visit them;—of women, who are charmed with you; I shall meet you at Lady Hartley's this evening.

So handsome a fellow as you are, so uncommon an understanding as you possess, such talents for repartee, such accomplishments, how can you bury your person and abilities in a mere family intercourse.

You are prodigiously sententious, Herbert.—All sentiment is now exploded, not only from conversation, but from the stage.—Even Cumberland's concise manner contains, I think, too strong a dose of soporific. The world is become too wise to receive advice—it is pedantic to give it.—Mirth, jollity, love, liberty, constitute the business of life.

Mrs. Herbert is, to be sure, a very fine woman—a sensible woman, a good wife, a fond mother, &c. &c.,—vastly well; these are the requisites for a domestic character, but you would wish to be a man of the world, Charles;—to have eyes for other women besides your wife, and she has a very proper sense of the submission becoming a wife. You tell me, she never attempts to confine you; she wishes you to please yourself. What the deuce makes the man so squeamish? She can work, and read, and write, and nurse, without you.

Come then, prithee meet me this evening, or I shall take it unkindly. I should have called on you, but I am beset with a parcel of unmeaning sycophants.

Your's most sincerely,

WILTON.

LETTER XXXIV.

To Lord Wilton.

YOU rally me, my Lord—you know my attachment to you, and your power over me, and you use it unmercifully.—You flatter me by ascribing to me superior abilities, yet tempt me to misapply them.— You have praised my heart. Why do you wish to mislead it? You laugh at me for sentiment and principle. But alas! the sentiments you attribute to me are not actuating principles? I have failed, not from the inefficacy of principle, but from my own irresolution, and want of exertion.

You do not render justice to the most amiable and excellent of her sex.—Yes, my Lord, I dare to assert that Mrs. Herbert, my wife, is one of the most amiable, and excellent of her sex.—"A fine woman, a sensible woman, a good wife, a fond mother." I have eyes for others, but I have a heart only for her. Her soul retains the image of its Creator. The brightness of her character has hitherto irradiated my path.

She has been the pole star of my conduct. Would to God she were still so! and that I were not benighted in the gloom of error.

Your description of her is cold and unanimated—it is applicable to many valuable women, but it is too faint for the delineation of my Caroline—I feel the influence of her perfections, but I feel also a degrading consciousness of my own demerits. Shall I then blush at hearing the senseless ridicule aimed at a connection which ought to constitute the happiness and glory of a rational being? Let me rather blush at my own misconduct.

I choose, my Lord, rather to write to you than to meet you. I have met you, and your parties too often. I acknowledge the accomplishments of the ladies you mention: they are pleasing, they are captivating, but why do they spread their snares for a married man? and why does your Lordship aid them by your dangerous reinforcements? Can the conjugal knot be dissolved? My heart, and duty, answer no! My soul is still devoted to my Caroline, and let me endeavour to render every future action of my life, subservient to her happiness.

I have too long slumbered on the brink of a precipice. I am now awake, and, while my faculties are unclouded, let me renounce every dangerous connection. You may despise my weakness. I feel and lament it. I trusted too much to my own strength.

With real sentiments of friendship,

     I remain,

          your Lordship's

             sincerely devoted,

                CHARLES HERBERT.

LETTER XXXV.

To Richard Brumpton, Esq.

I KNOW not what to make of Herbert. He is the most squeamish, sentimental mortal I ever met with. I invited him to be of our party at Lady Hartley's, but he sent me a refusal, with his rule of life in select sentences.

I can talk with him, when surrounded by a gay assembly, or I can laugh him out of countenance, when I have nothing to say; but the fellow draws his pen upon me, foils me desperately at this weapon, and quite disables me.

It must be upon the weakness of his resolution, or rather upon the milkiness of his disposition, that I must work.—A sad tale engages all his attention. I will introduce him to two seeming objects of compassion. William and Sally Marston, shall be the pretended sufferers:—reduced to indigence by the villainy of a guardian, who has escaped into another country.—I have not yet planned the whole of the story, but I can make it a deplorable one; and, lest he should suspect my design, I choose to have a brother sufferer as well as a sister.

The fellow is shrewd and suspicious—and so extremely attached to his wife.—I hate to hear her praises from his mouth or pen.—I must lower him—lessen his internal confidence. Pride he has none, for he is so foolish as to be unassuming, and even timid; but he preserves too much the dignity of action and character.

Come to me, Brumpton, and we will concert the means of debasing him. Come instantly.

Your's,

WILTON.

LETTER XXXVI.

To Mr. Berkeley.

My dear Son,

YOU will be, perhaps, surprised to find I am no stranger to Mr. Herbert's conduct. The reports I heard excited my apprehensions. I requested Miss Herbert to acquaint me with the truth. I dared not apply to you, fearing I might say too much on the affecting subject, and either add to the resentment you must feel, if the informations were just, or awaken suspicions to Mr. Herbert's prejudice, if they proved groundless.

You will pity my fears rather than be displeased with this effect of them; for, I find, I might have trusted you. Your moderation increases my love for you, whilst your ineffectual remonstrances with Mr. Herbert redouble my affliction—Persevere, my dear son, in that calmness, which I applaud.—Endeavour to restore him to your sister by mild expostulations. Remember his former exalted character; and that his weakness claims the support of friendship. Do not aggravate your sister's wrongs by an attempt to revenge them. I charge you on my blessing always to preserve that happy disposition which has hitherto been the guide of your actions.

Mr. Herbert is not an abandoned libertine. Example, and want of resolution, rather than inclination, have drawn him from the path of duty. My daughter's merit, your prudence, and his own principles, will restore him to virtue. He will soon despise the society in which he now delights, and himself for being capable of relishing their amusements. Believe me, he will suffer more pain from conviction of his delusion, and the miseries it has occasioned, than your reproaches can inflict.—I hope the happy time is not far distant when you will embrace the sincere penitent; and sooth his mind to a forgiveness of its own errors.—But I need say no more.—Your heart is your best monitor.

I hardly know whether grief for my daughter's affliction, or admiration of her virtues, is predominant in my breast. Both are inexpressible!—God grant I may never have occasion to renew this subject!—In your happiness, and my dear daughter's, is included that of

your ever affectionate mother,

ELIZABETH BERKELEY.

LETTER XXXVII.

To Mrs. Berkeley.

HOW strongly, dear madam, does the tenderness of the mother animate every line of your letter! I have long felt for my sister and myself. I now severely feel for you. What an interruption to that happiness, which I hoped would have been as permanent as it was perfect.—But, while I blame my brother's conduct, my heart is wounded by his sufferings.

He has renewed an acquaintance with a Lord Wilton. Captivated by his conversation, my unguarded friend too easily admitted him to his bosom.—Finding, I fear, by experience, that he had too precipitately engaged in an intimacy, he became dissatisfied and uneasy. Yet, instead of abandoning Wilton, he is only grown more cautious in mentioning him, and invites him less frequently to his house. His friendship for me seems to be cooled. He shuns my company. When we meet, his constrained looks convince me that he fears reproaches, which he is conscious of deserving; yet, fascinated by Lord Wilton, he cannot give up an acquaintance who has deprived him of his happiness. If I mention his Caroline, whose exalted merit claims an eternal constancy, he joins me with heartfelt warmth; yet his blushes tacitly confess an humiliating consciousness. I have intreated him to avoid an intimacy with Lord Wilton, and by degrees to give up the acquaintance. That wretch is now out of town with a sick uncle, from whom he has great expectations. I begged my brother would determine to see him no more; but he enjoined me silence. He cannot defend, he tells me, every particular of Lord Wilton's character, but he has obligations to him which he must conceal, and which prevent his declining the acquaintance. What can these obligations be? My anxiety is equal to my friendship for him, and affection to my sister.

Every face in the family is changed, and every heart is engrossed by some uneasiness which it attempts to conceal.—My sister, my amiable sister, shews only by her altered looks the disorder of her mind.—In her, the tender wife, the fond mother, suffers!

Miss Herbert is deeply interested in the cause of friendship. She feels for the anxiety of the wife, the anguish of the mother. She condemns the infatuation, whilst she pities the weakness of the husband, but, I believe, her compassion and admiration of her sister, excite stronger emotions of resentment towards her brother than pity for his self-inflicted sufferings can subdue.

Miss Woodford (I scarcely dare to call her my Clara) is also altered.—That easy frankness, which heightened my esteem, though it did not perfectly satisfy my love, seems to have given place to a gloomy fretfulness.—But we are involved in one general calamity.

Be not apprehensive, dear madam, that passion should prompt me to revenge my sister, nor that even love can render me insensible to the dictates of friendship. I know, I pity Mr. Herbert.—Yes, I am convinced with you, that much more severe must be the anguish he feels on reflection, than that which he inflicts. I will endeavour to regain him by such methods only as your goodness advises.

Comfort yourself, dearest madam, by indulging that favourable opinion you wish to inspire in me.—My sister's cause is the cause of heaven, and her triumph will be aided by its assistance. Trust me, this superior instance of her virtue will more firmly cement their union.

Be assured, that, whatever be our situation, nothing can weaken the duty and affection of

your ever obedient,

and gratefully affectionate son,

HENRY BERKELEY.

LETTER XXXVIII.

To Richard Brumpton, Esq.

COULD you have imagined, Brumpton, that a fellow so lively, so attached to pleasure as I am, could support a tedious confinement in the sick room of an old wretch, whose recovery I dread, and whom I wish at rest in his grave? But you know my inducement.—His lands, tenements, and hereditaments, will amply repay my attendance. The farce is almost over. The last scene is opened to my view, and the curtain will soon drop.

By my faith, Brumpton, it will be some time, I doubt, before the risible muscles of my face will be capable of resuming their functions; yet I have a happy facility in adapting my appearance to persons and times. My uncle thinks me a saint; I fear, if he is destined to be one in Heaven, he will have a very different opinion of his nephew. I could hasten his last moment, by acquainting him with my real character, and the swift circulation I shall make of those pretty pieces he has been so long collecting—but that would be dangerous work, ha! Dick.—I have often thought it a happy circumstance that the old Don lives so far from London. He would else hear strange stories of his kinsman—little akin, I doubt, in heart.

Prithee, good Captain, take care of Herbert; let me not lose my prey;—the fellow deserves to suffer for his romantic confidence. Who but himself would have permitted so charming a creature as his wife, to be frequently seen by a hare-um-scare-um Lord, mad in the pursuit of pleasure?

You will say he did not thoroughly know my character. Character, simpleton! People seldom have occasion to make enquiries of noblemen at my time of life. Surely I am not worse than most of my age and rank. Do you think I am? That's some comfort, Dick! though, I doubt, that excuse would be insufficient with my uncle—hardly do, I fancy. But I shall reform some time hence.

The Wife; or, Caroline Herbert

Hark ye, Brumpton! let not Herbert be much at home—haunt him; suffer him not to see his wife if possible; for I am terribly afraid my absence may prove destructive to my hopes. I believe he loves me.— That rencounter at Sally's lodgings, in which I appeared to be his protector against an unequal assault, I think has secured him. Yet how bitterly did he lament being seduced by that artful girl! how did she work upon his unsuspecting confidence! He even wept at her narration; and his pity led him into the snare I had prepared to awaken his passions.

But never will he forgive himself—and, if he knew the use I intend to make of his conduct, he never could forgive me.

He was ashamed to see his wife.—The society, into which I introduced him, diverted, in some measure, his attention from thoughts that almost distracted him.—The longer he continues in this course of life, the more difficult it will be to break the chain, which unites him to us.

This from you, Wilton! methinks I hear you say. Even so, Brumpton. I am not blind to reason, though she casts but a dim light into my breast. Pleasure, my boy, pleasure is my goddess! I have long bowed before her shrine, and she has not a more obsequious votary. I cannot say she has sufficiently repaid my adorations, but hope enlivens me, and even disappointment cannot wholly dispirit me.

This woman, this beautiful, this enchanting Caroline, has occasioned me more uneasy moments than I ever felt before—she certainly thinks not so well of me as her husband does—a cold civility has been the best reception I ever experienced from her, but of late she deprives me even of this, and leaves the room immediately on my entrance.

I cannot bear it, Dick.—I, who doat upon the sex, to be treated in this manner by one whom I prefer to all the rest! She is almost the only female who has mortified my vanity. My conquests are indeed, in general, too easy. I have not the pleasure of surmounting a difficulty.—Mrs. Herbert seems to promise me much trouble; but I care not, if I can at last prove successful.

She loves her husband, you say; but can he love this most admirable woman? When I mention the charms of her person, he launches out in praises of the beauties of her mind.—When I admire the easy politeness of her behaviour, he cries, O! she is of an

angelic disposition.—Her mind, indeed! give me her person, and I am satisfied.—He once told me, my description of her was cold and unanimated.—He little thinks how much I endeavoured to smother the warmth that glowed in my heart, to prevent its flaming to my pen.

Her disposition too! she is not of that pliable temper I wish her to be—yet, faith, I know not whether I could adore an inanimate symmetry of form; and perhaps to that sweetness which smiles upon her features, they may owe a great part of their enchanting loveliness. Shall I rob her of her most engaging charm?

I know not whether I shall be able to subdue this haughty fair, but I cannot, will not resign my hopes. Besides, I have another scheme.— But you shall know nothing of it unless I succeed.

The old gentleman is awake, and calls me to him. Adieu! Captain. Remember your instructions, and acquit yourself of this commission in a manner that may entitle you to farther commands from your's,

WILTON.

LETTER XXXIX.

To Mrs. Berkeley.

Dear Madam,

I CAN readily allow for the first emotions of your resentment against my wretched brother. We continue in much the same unhappy way.

Miss Woodford has left us for a few weeks, and is gone to her cousin Bennet. My beloved sister and I mingle our tears, but reproaches are all my own. She trusts in that all-gracious Being who never deserts the innocent, and who will recompense the sufferings which he permits. Her soul rises superior to its woes, while hope opens to her a prospect of everlasting happiness. Human nature must feel, but Christianity triumphs. You, my dear madam, enjoy the same resources which your Caroline draws from this fountain of life.

May my poor deceived brother derive benefit and consolation from those principles, by which now, alas! he ceases to be actuated, that we may become as happy by his reformation as we are now made miserable by his deviation.

I am

dear madam,

most respectfully and affectionately

your's,

LUCIA HERBERT.

END OF VOL. I

VOLUME II

LETTER XL.

To Mrs. Herbert.

THE conversation which passed between us the day before I left town, has opened my eyes to the view of a danger, I never before apprehended.

Tell me, dearest Mrs. Herbert, tell me, do you not think I have fatally indulged—what can I say? O most excellent of women, your penetration has searched the inmost recesses of my heart.—I am alarmed, terrified—but I wish, I intreat you to shew me to myself. I have been cherishing a docile spirit. Impetuous and uncontroullable by nature, I am become a convert to your sweetness.

Be so kind as to favour immediately with an answer,

Your obliged and affectionate

CLARA WOODFORD.

LETTER XLI.

To Miss Woodford.

WITH what a noble frankness do you call upon me, my dear Miss Woodford, to disclose to you the secret foldings of your heart! I will be ingenuous.

I have for some time suspected that you indulged love, where you believed you only nourished gratitude and friendship. I have pitied you, and wished to assist you in overcoming a passion more fatal to your peace, than to my repose.

You understand me, my dear, my generous friend.—A fancied security too often deceives us into real danger. Gratitude insensibly betrays an unwary heart into more tender sentiments.—Ah! my love, we cannot be too strict and constant in the examination of ourselves.

Consider, my sweet friend:—A young lady, who wishes to decline marrying a worthy man, because she has a high esteem for the husband of another woman, ought to suspect the rectitude of her intentions. If she really felt only esteem, what should prevent her from entering into an engagement, where love and esteem must blend to form a perfect union?

The man, my Clara, who solicits you to make him happy, is allowed to be not only respectable, but amiable. You once acknowledged him to be so. You seemed to be sensible of his merit. Yet this man you have for some time delighted to teaze; while, with an unguarded earnestness, you have sought to attract the attention of another, that other, the husband of your friend; of one who not only depends on his fidelity, but his kindness, for all her temporal happiness.

Be not displeased with me, my sweet ward, my friend, my sister (if you will allow me the endearing tie); does not your heart answer to these tender admonitions? When I distantly touched on the interesting subject, your glowing cheek, your downcast eye, confessed you made the application. You retired with an abruptness that confirmed my fears. You shunned me; you chose to accompany Mrs. Bennet down; but your letter, my beloved friend, eases my mind of all its fears, and increases towards you my esteem and love.

Heaven be praised that you feel and condemn an error, which, though it had its source in gratitude and esteem, might have been productive of the most dreadful consequences, of mental, if not of actual, guilt. Rapid, though imperceptible, are the progressions of vice.

But do you not think, my dear Miss Woodford, that I usurp an authority you meant not to delegate? You solicited me to disclose my sentiments, but have I not been too explicit? I disclaim any superior degree of penetration in discerning this small speck in your character.—Your unguarded looks, and behaviour, my love, laid you open to observation; especially to the observation of an interested spectator; but a boasted penetration is more frequently the proof of a bad heart, than of a distinguishing head.

They, who are free from the faults of others, will most probably find on examination, some bosom failing, which renders them equally culpable. I believe that those who are nearest perfection, will always be found capable of the most exalted tenderness and compassion.— thankful to heaven for assisting their perseverance, they will neither feel their vanity raised, nor their severity excited by comparison with the frailty of others. What! shall human imperfections dare to become a rigid censor on a fellow-creature's infirmity?

Assure me, my beloved Miss Woodford, of your forgiveness? May I again venture to address you in the admonitory strain? Deprive me not of your regard; for you have not a more sincere, nor affectionate friend, than

Your

CAROLINE HERBERT..

LETTER XLII.

To Mrs. Berkeley.

HOW amazingly, my dear Madam, do some people trifle away their happiness! That Mrs. Fenning, whom I last year attended as a bride, is become quite the fashionable wife.

Is it not astonishing that any person should solicit the acquaintance of another, and yet receive no benefit from her example. From such an example as my sister? Mrs. Fenning is married to a very worthy man, one who relishes her vivacity, but dislikes her levity.

We called yesterday at the house of this lady, (who is but lately returned to town from her country seat), and were greatly surprised at the reception we met with, and at Mrs. Fenning's appearance.— She was slatternly dressed, her hair was dishevelled, her eyes were swelled with weeping; yet her tears seemed to be the effusion of resentment rather than of sorrow, and her face glowed with passion.

Our amazement keeping us silent, "Dear creatures," said she, (raising herself from a sofa, on which she reclined when we entered,) "this is very kind, but I am ashamed to be seen by you in such a dishabille; yet, as I did not expect company, you will think it excusable."

"I hope you are well, Madam," answered my sister; "for this disorder in your dress and looks makes me apprehensive for you." "Oh! child," cried Mrs. Fenning, "I have had such a lecture this morning! Would you believe it? Mr. Fenning has been accusing me of wasting time in dress when I am to appear in public, and neglecting a proper attention to neatness and decency when I am at home with him.

"Can any thing be so unreasonable? Does he think I am to employ my time in adorning myself to please a husband? Preposterous! Of what importance is it, now we are married?

"He tells me, I am not the same woman to whom he paid his addresses.—But he should be sensible we then both acted a part, and that now the assumed character is laid aside.—Would not a reasonable man be pleased to have his wife admired, whenever she goes abroad?

"How could the antiquated notions of neatness and decency enter his head? A fine lady is not confined to the rules of the vulgar! Neatness and decency may be proper enough for tradesmen's wives, but the polite break through these narrow limits.—A groveling wretch! What can be more mortifying? To dress for a husband? What person of fashion ever did such a thing?"

Here her tears interrupted her harangue; and my sister's answer excited in her equal surprise with that she had inspired in us. "Will you forgive me, Madam," said she, "if my opinion differs from yours? But, I beg pardon, you are certainly in jest when you say you only acted a part; indeed, were the latter the case, your good sense must convince you it is still necessary to keep up the assumed character, as you call it, unless you wish to disturb domestic harmony.—Mr. Fenning has a right, you know, to expect your utmost endeavours to please him, and surely those endeavours must constitute your highest happiness."

"A right! Mrs. Herbert," interrupted the enraged lady; "I know not what you mean! This is new doctrine indeed. What! is he to control me in every thing?—To lay down rules for my dress, company, &c.; and am I to submit to his imperial will and pleasure? No, no:—I am not to be his slave. He shall know my spirit is not to be subdued, and if he persists in his attempts to contradict me, he will provoke an altercation, which may not perhaps conduce to his advantage."

"You may possibly think, Madam," replied my sister, "our short acquaintance does not authorize my freedom; but I assure you, that real concern for your neglected happiness influences me to hazard a remark. Can you think that this state of altercation is conformable to the design of the marriage union? Do you delight to render uneasy, a person to whom you have so solemnly vowed an obedience, which love would also dictate? Can you expect to be happy whilst you neglect an obvious and plighted duty?"

"Obedience! Duty!" cried Mrs. Fenning. "Are these sounds to be perpetually ringing in our ears? Perhaps they may be found in the matrimonial service, but the men made the law, and then they expect us only to keep it.—Let me ask you a question.—Do you receive from your husband the return of gratitude you ought to expect from your submission?"

I could not help exclaiming, "I look in vain for my old companion and friend in Mrs. Fenning. I am astonished, I am shocked at the alteration.

My sister struggled to disperse a little appearance of confusion.— "Indeed, Madam," answered she, with amazing composure, "I act not from a desire of inspiring gratitude; Mr. Herbert's esteem and affection repay my tenderness."

"Ah! Mrs. Herbert, Mrs. Herbert," cried Mrs. Fenning, with an eagerness which expressed triumph, "report says otherwise; and I am afraid with certainty—why do you conceal his folly?"

"And why do you, Madam," answered I, with the utmost warmth, "suggest a suspicion, which, in a jealous breast, would soon grow into conviction? It is cruel and ungenerous!—Were my brother really forgetful of his duty, by ignorance alone, could my sister preserve a state of tranquillity.—Who would officiously withdraw a veil which might conceal a spectacle of horror? Were she even conscious of such a misfortune, would it not be doubly distressing that what she would wish to bury in oblivion, should be disclosed to the world?"

"Well," interrupted Mrs. Fenning, "we are not likely to agree. I have no notion of these refinements. Let me be flattered and admired, let me enjoy the delightful satisfaction of shining in the drawing room, at the concert, or the ball, and I can willingly endure the occasional loss of a husband's good humour. I enjoy teazing him sometimes.— We differ in every particular but in the choice of separate amusements. I allow, indeed, he is not covetous, and you perhaps might think him reasonable, but I cannot bear contradiction, and I will not."

"Take care, Madam," cried my sister, "lest you provoke him too far."

"Oh! dear Madam," replied the other, "you are infinitely kind. Permit me to give you a piece of advice in return.—Try to awaken your husband's jealousy, by encouraging some admirer's passion.— Mrs. Herbert's beauty claims universal adoration, and when Mr. Herbert finds himself singular in his neglect of you, I do not doubt but you will regain his affection."

"No, Madam," answered my amiable sister, "were I as miserable as you insinuate, I would not be so guilty as you advise me to be.—I would not part from the conscious integrity of my heart, even to recover a husband's love. The woman, who preserves her husband's esteem, may flatter herself with the hope of being re-established in his affection; but when esteem is lost, love cannot be regained.—But this conversation has been carried too far. You will permit us therefore to drop the subject, and to take our leave," which we did with little ceremony.

What say you, Madam, to this woman? I blush for her.—Modish manners have ruined a friendly, though gay heart. Unhappy creature! How I admire my sister's virtues and circumspection! But the conduct of the one is as much beneath criticism, as the sentiments and behaviour of the other are superior to all praise.

I am happy in my alliance to such merit, and earnestly wish she had not reason to lament it.—Permit me to add, that I have a high degree of satisfaction in subscribing myself an admirer and humble imitator of your virtues, and that I am

Your faithful and affectionate,

LUCIA HERBERT.

LETTER XLIII.

To Charles Herbert, Esq.

Dear Herbert,

THE greatest mortification I feel in being confined to the country arises from my absence from you: I doubt you are not sufficiently sensible of this truth.—They tell me you are become thoughtful and melancholy.—Surely that foolish affair cannot still render you uneasy.

Clear up, Charles—disperse the clouds that overspread your brow, and let the sun of mirth and good humour shine forth again—frequent our society—there admiration waits you—all are prepared to entertain you—Brumpton will attend you, and supply my place. If, as you say, you consider yourself obliged to me, follow my advice, chase away desponding thoughts, and avoid company that will infect you.

I hear Berkeley threatens me, for drawing you away from home.— But sure you have cast away your leading strings—or are you still a baby?—If so, confine yourself to the nursery.—A wife and puling infant are fit company for a pusillanimous, meek-spirited husband.—But you are more of a man—shake off entirely the unnatural subjection—exert yourself, and be master of your own inclinations and family.

Your wife, I suppose, has complained to her brother; and is this a proof of the duty you think she so steadily practises? No, no, Charles, she is but a woman, though I really believe her to be one of the best.

Do not indulge thought—I shall soon be in town, and will put you in a method to become as gay, and lively as

Your faithful

WILTON.

LETTER XLIV.

Mr. Herbert to Lord Wilton.

OH! thou destroyer of my peace! Do you still continue to torment me? Shall I never taste of happiness again? Take from me, then, that power of reflection, which only heightens my misery, by comparing the present with the past!—On the future I hardly dare to turn my thoughts!

Great God! to what a society have I abandoned myself. I never think without being sensible of the degradation! But, instead of seeking to recover the path of virtue, I have wandered with other vagrants in the labyrinths of vice.

How have I fallen from the summit of earthly felicity, to a state below the dignity of man! I was sensible of my first deviation. Remorse assailed me—I blushed for myself, but I afterwards blushed, because the companions that diverted an idle hour, laughed at my scrupulous exactness.—I was ashamed of being happy!

My wife!—but I scarcely dare to think of her.—It is too painful a remembrance; yet you have presumed to insinuate that my Caroline betrayed me to her brother.—'Tis false, Wilton!—She never complained—she bears my faults with patience—her love for me continues unaltered. But I see that pity mingles with it, and I am a wretch to abuse such goodness.

What a return have I made!—Oh! why did you save my life, when you had betrayed my honour?—It was your barbarous triumph over my reason, which made me first forget my Caroline!—And when I forgot her, I lost all remembrance of my duty!

Shall the hours of blissful conversation, shall the time of delightful reflection never more recur?—Ah! no:—riotous mirth, distracting thoughts, have usurped their place. Could I recall the past, I should still be happy!

The Wife; or, Caroline Herbert

Would to God I had never known you, or that we had never resumed our acquaintance!—Why did you intrude on my unguarded, unsuspecting heart?—You were a witness of the happiness which you have destroyed.—But why do I blame you?—I best knew my own happiness, and the treasure I had to keep or abandon. You tempted me, indeed, but the fault was my own; I trusted too much to my own power of resisting temptation, because I loved my Caroline, because I had been enabled to perform some of the duties of life.

I had proved the sweets of the most perfect union, heaven ever sanctified.—I had nothing more to wish—I wanted not a friend.— My wife was my bosom friend—my companion—my guardian angel.—A little cherub had blessed us with an increase of delight.— What fiend induced me to seek for pleasure abroad, when I enjoyed the most exalted happiness at home?

You, Lord Wilton, were the demon, who assumed an engaging appearance to tempt a weak wretch to the purposes of hell.—I am almost distracted—I cannot think—yet mention not my wife as you have dared to mention her.

Surely I have laid aside my leading strings, you say:—no, Wilton, you have led me to my destruction. When I wandered from my duty, I ceased to be a man, and became weaker than an infant. I struggled awhile, but the superiority of your cunning, triumphed over the weakness of my efforts, and I submitted at last to your guidance.

Why did I ever loosen the silken chain, that gently led my steps in the path of virtue?—Shame and remorse pursue me.—An injured wife, whose tears only have reproached me—a helpless infant, whose weakness demands my tenderness and protection—these dear objects awaken dreadful reflections, nor can all your boasted gaiety lull me again to forgetfulness.

Why must I be troubled with the impertinence of Brumpton?—I flattered myself, when you were absent, I should recover my peace.—But it will not be—solitude can afford no tranquillity to one, who wishes to banish thought. He who enjoys it, must be able to look backward without self-reproach, and forward without apprehension.

This meek-spirited, this pusillanimous husband, as you insultingly call me, is not a proper inmate of that nursery, to which you would confine him. That sweet abode of peace and innocence, is too pure for so unworthy a guest.

The joy that sparkles in my Caroline's eyes, when she beholds me, the smiles of my little infant, upbraid me more cruelly than the severest reproaches.—I can scarcely support their sight—the looks of my sister express the most friendly resentment; and indeed she has more than once hinted her displeasure.—Mr. Berkeley has gently expostulated with me.

Have I reason to be angry?—Far, far otherwise.—It is love for my wife that influences their conduct, whilst mine appears to be actuated by a contrary motive.—Yet, could they know my heart, they would find it filled with the most sincere affection man ever felt.

Why can I not disclose it?—I am ashamed to own myself convinced of an error—is it not so?—Foolish wretch! False grounded shame!—Let me confide in that faithful bosom, which will perhaps communicate to me the serenity it enjoys, and calm my troubled soul.

But you have said, it must not be—my own honour and my obligations to you forbid it!—Why, Wilton, why did you preserve a life hateful to me, and which has destroyed the peace of others? If you would reconcile me to it, hasten to town, release me from those obligations, and permit me to renounce a society, in whose circle is contagion, and whose end is ruin.

At present, there is not a wretch more miserable than

CHARLES HERBERT.

LETTER XLV.

To Lord Wilton.

My Lord,

AS I assisted you during your absence from town, I expect you will bear with what you may deem my impertinence, and even facilitate my scheme by your advice.

A new scene opens:—the characters are Miss Forest, an amiable young lady, and sole heiress to £30,000. and Captain Brumpton, a fellow who dresses well, talks fashionably, and has made conquests of half the women in town.

The day after I came into the country, I accidentally met this lady on a visit.—She is really handsome, and her dress, though not fashionable, I must confess is very becoming.—She gave me a proof of her understanding, by distinguishing me, in a particular manner, from the boors who were present.

I enquired into her fortune, had a satisfactory account, and was not discouraged by hearing she has formed her expectation of a lover from romances.—A sort of reading to which I never applied—nor to any study, you will say, but how to partake the gaieties of fashionable life.

Her father is a parson, who married a woman of very large fortune, and she left only this child. Mr. Forest's character, however, somewhat allayed my assurance of success; but a servant, whom I found means to corrupt, informed me, her lady's affections might be gained by respectful assiduities, and that to conceal my love will be the most certain method to meet with a return.

By the contrivance of this maid, I have sometimes seen the fair Henrietta, and have so well improved my opportunities, that she regards me with all the complacency which I can expect.

The Wife; or, Caroline Herbert

I ran over the whole vocabulary of Cupid's inspiration.—I told her all Nature wore its brightest aspect when she appeared—that the envious roses blushed to find themselves so far excelled by the bloom on her cheeks, and the coral on her lips—that her eyes eclipsed the lustre of the sun, that the zephyrs pressed to steal a kiss, that—but I cannot repeat all the nonsense with which I have assailed her heart—you will laugh at this short sketch of my courtship.

I have had a great deal of trouble—I have sat up three or four nights, reading the Grand Cyrus, Clelia, Cleopatra, and Cassandra. Did not her fortune incite me, this girl had never tasted the satisfaction of receiving from me an heroic address.

Next week her father carries her to town, where his attendance is required in consequence of a law-suit. I shall precipitate an explanation, lest her fortune should raise me any formidable rivals.

Her father, you will tell me, may render my hopes abortive, by refusing to resign this fortune.—Why, truly, my Lord, I should be rather fearful of consequences, (for a wife is to me an unnecessary appendage,) but my rural lass has £10,000. independent of him, left by an uncle. This will enable me to support her father's resentment, if the old curmudgeon should be inflexible.

But I must conclude abruptly; for I have several tedious pages of Artamenes to turn over. You shall soon receive another letter from

      Your's sincerely,

      RICHARD BRUMPTON.

LETTER XLVI.

To Mrs. Herbert.

O MADAM, why cannot I express my gratitude and love! I can only tell you they equal your goodness. How nobly does your practice evince the truth of your assertion, that those nearest perfection are most capable of exalted tenderness and compassion. You have acquired a right to censure infirmities, from which you are entirely free; yet how tenderly have you exercised it—but you are *all perfection*.

Happy am I that you discovered me to myself! I had often asked my heart, why it was so insensible to your goodness, which yet I could not help acknowledging, and why it was so favourably disposed to Mr. Herbert, who was less kind than you?—I sighed at the retrospect, yet still imagined my dislike could proceed from no other cause than your severe virtue.

The basis of my affection for Mr. Herbert was esteem.—I admired the uniform tenor of his conduct.—His unremitted tenderness towards you was the principal circumstance that engaged my regard for him; yet, alas! it had an undue influence upon my heart. His absence shocked me, but (inconsistent! horrid! detestable passion!) my concern was mingled with somewhat of a guilty gratification, on finding your society was not so very essential to his happiness, as I had concluded it to be. Gracious Heaven! I am disgusted, frightened, on the review of this dangerous attachment.

When Lady D—— endeavoured to withdraw Mr. Herbert from you, and attract him to herself, I felt less alarmed than incensed at her supposing him to be capable of being seduced by any personal charms, from his love and duty; yet I afterwards wished (deceitful, vile heart!) to give a softer turn to his esteem for me, than was consistent with his solemnly plighted vows, and love for you.

What chimerical scheme of felicity had I formed. I determined never to marry—I imagined I could live happy with Mr. Herbert, as a friend.—Alas! I find I rather listened to the suggestion of love than to the pleadings of virtue and reason.—You, madam, have restored me to both! I am calm, and tolerably reconciled to myself.

I esteem Mr. Herbert, but I no longer love him.—I begin to be truly sensible of Mr. Berkeley's merit, and to hope it will be in my power to reward it. For you, madam, my heart feels inexpressible sentiments of gratitude and love.

Be not apprehensive, best of friends, of disclosing all that is upon your mind. From your pen flow the purest, the most exalted dictates of the human heart. I expect, I require from you the most explicit confidence. My heart shall be open to your inspection; you shall explore every secret fold, its every shadow of a wish.—You cannot offend me but by making apologies.

Believe me, most excellent of women, no one can more truly feel for you the sentiments of love, esteem, and admiration, than

your ever gratefully affectionate

CLARA WOODFORD.

LETTER XLVII.

To Richard Brumpton, Esq.

IF the love-sick Oroondates can awhile forbear to gaze on the bright eyes of the divine Statira: if, on withdrawing his view from those celestial luminaries, he is not involved in the mists of darkness, an humble swain requests him to peruse this epistle.—I cannot proceed—but that will do for you, Dick—I wrote it merely for your instruction.

Why what an army have you to encounter! "Gorgons, and hydras, and chimeras dire."—So this fair one is entrenched behind a huge rampart of massy folios. Will you find sufficient ammunition to maintain the siege?—This kind of attack is quite new to you.

Well, thanks to the god of love, I have nothing to read but the minds of my charmers; and let me tell you I sometimes find them obscure books, for there are so many editions, with considerable alterations, and no emendations, that I am frequently at a loss to decypher the meaning; but it is much easier than to encounter your adversaries.

Mercy on us, Brumpton! what a wild-goose chase are you entered upon! You will find it much more difficult to obtain this £30,000. than Oroondates or Artaban did to vanquish the same number of men.

Now to my own affairs, which by the bye, you had not the grace to mention,—not a word of consolation to a poor fellow, who stands in so much need of it.—Your love absorbed all your thoughts.—Not the love of woman, however; it was love of yourself, Captain, that had engrossed you.

I am horridly out of humour with my old gentleman. To be confined to his sick room so long—for no purpose agreeable to me.—I fear my presence hastened his recovery. Then to be forced to congratulate his return of health, at which all my hopes sickened—I hurried up to town on pretence of business, and left the old usurer to add to the golden hoard.

I have scarcely seen Herbert.—I fear he lives too much at home; and methinks his charming wife wears an air of ease that does not suit my designs upon her. I must disturb this harmony. I think I have the means.

I met Miss Herbert in company yesterday, where you were mentioned.—"What an odd compound," said she, "is Captain Brumpton! he is a fop, yet not devoid of wit.—Indeed he has so much, that, when he converses only with his own sex, one would not suspect he pays such attention to his pretty person; but, when with our's, he shews, that in his own supposed perfections all his happiness centers; and that he estimates the understanding of others, by the approbation they shew of him."

You are an odd fellow, Dick!—I think the girl judges too favourably of you, for I have frequently thought and called you an insignificant puppy. Perhaps it is vanity that makes me assume an appearance of regard for you, and some other insects of your tribe—a desire to shew my own superiority. You have too much vanity, and are too well acquainted with my sincerity, to suspect me of truth.

Well! be is as it may—I believe we are equally capable of friendship.—I do not flatter you, Captain;—write again—perhaps I may answer your letter—but, if not, you know it is your duty to obey—and, to encourage you, I will confess, I really believe I feel some affection for you.—When the Arcadian plains surrender up their guest, you may possibly be again serviceable to your

WILTON.

LETTER XLVIII.

To Lord Wilton.

YOUR letter, my Lord, does not so much prove your disappointment as your independence. None but a man of your fortunes, could write with that elegant spirit, that flowing negligence.—You do not seem to want consolation, yet I beg pardon for my forgetfulness.

Matters here go on swimmingly.—The little rustic is my own.— Apropos—I have purchased a new suit. It is in the height of the mode.—My rogue of a taylor refused me credit, till I assured him I was on the brink of marriage with a very rich heiress.—No more hesitation, you may believe.

But what a lover you are, methinks I hear you say, to make so quick a transition from the conquest of a blooming fair one, to a new coat. Perhaps, with Miss Herbert, you may think me too much of a fop— but outside appearance, my Lord, has more effect than some may imagine on the heart of every woman, even where the predominant passion is not vanity, which reigns supreme in the hearts of most of the sex. I believe my fair romancer is not insensible to this kind of merit. Dress is the study of the sex, and they are pleased with the taste of their lovers.

I am a happy man, my Lord. The frowns of beauty cannot disconcert me, nor her smiles transport me beyond the bounds of reason. In the former case, I condemn her want of judgment; and in the latter, am only exalted into an higher opinion of my own merit—an ingenuous confession, is it not, and which hardly contradicts Miss Herbert's observation.

I shall soon bid an entire adieu to want and my shabby wardrobe. Did I tell you Mr. Forest is a clergyman?—he is, faith! and if he suspected me, would most probably read me a lecture, for he is a very eloquent advocate on the side of priestcraft.

You have sent a fine specimen of your knight-errantry—I am sometimes at a loss—my memory is deficient,—I have read enough to furnish me with materials for gaining all the romantic girls in Christendom.—Such absurdity!—Could I but obtain £30,000. by any other means, Henrietta might bless some more worthy swain with her regard.—But the time of meeting draws near, and I have not sufficiently conned my lesson. I am vapoured with the thoughts of my task.

Adieu, my Lord. I believe I shall resign my commission when I marry: for it is a disagreeable circumstance to be subjected to the commands of a superior officer: yet, on consideration, I may be glad of a pretence to quit my wife; a golden chain will not reconcile me to the loss of liberty.—What can sound more shocking than the married

DICK BRUMPTON.

LETTER XLIX.

To Miss Woodford.

My dearest Clara,

IT is only a great mind that will acknowledge, with gratitude, the justness of reproof: a mean soul will rather defend than own a mistake. It resents accusations it is not ashamed to deserve, and, instead of atoning for a past error, incurs farther guilt, by rejecting the admonitions of friendship.

I congratulate you, on your delightful change.—Persevere, my love, and you will secure present happiness, and eternal felicity. I, my dear, am but the instrument of your conviction.—To Heaven you owe gratitude, adoration, love, and obedience. Let neither business nor pleasure render you forgetful of your duty.—God does not extend his grace to those who depend wholly on him without the exertion of their own powers, nor will he assist any, who rely entirely on their own strength. It must be our constant endeavour to do good, and resist evil, joined with fervent prayer to Heaven for assistance, which can alone support a lively Christian hope of divine acceptance.

You own, my dear, that you have indulged some dangerous propensities. Did not your turn of reading rather enervate your mind? You have often talked of nourishing a pure Platonic flame. Ah! my Clara, a Platonic flame is generally mixed with drossy particles. True piety is uniform and consistent. You have felt that the real heroine is she who resists the approaches of guilt whatever shape it assumes, however flattering its appearance.

I have heard you speak too lightly of matrimonial obligations. Do not human ordinances, instituted for public utility, receive the divine sanction?—They infringe the duty of Christian benevolence, who speak or think with levity of ceremonies which cement the virtue and happiness of social intercourse.

Consider, my dear, the influence of your gay conversation, and free opinions.—The libertine, whose oaths are prostituted to every woman who pleases him, will not reflect that his insincerity is offensive to Heaven, and his example prejudicial to the world, but will plead your opinion in defence of his practice. Could you support the thought of having contributed to the sufferings of innocence and the success of villainy? I am certain you would not: you want only a little more consideration, to distinguish between dangerous levity, and innocent cheerfulness.

How severely, my dear friend, did you condemn the frailty of Miss L——. Unaccustomed to any restraint of her inclinations, bred up in luxury, and never pinched by the severe hand of penury, she was terrified at its appearance. She saw no alternative, but to submit to poverty, or, by relinquishing the sweets of innocence, to preserve the splendid trappings of prodigality. Her fears prevailed, and she was miserable. The evil she attempted to shun, still haunted her.—Again affrighted, she again became guilty, and is now the wretched victim of that sex by whom she was adored.

Tell me, my dear, do not the circumstances that betrayed her, somewhat alleviate the heinousness of her guilt?—Should we not be rigidly severe in self-examination, conscious of the fallibility of our own hearts, and soften the asperity of judgment, on the faults of others.—Shall not the tear of pity fall for the weakness of human nature?

Indelicacy of sentiment more easily insinuates itself into the heart, concealed under the specious name of gaiety, than when it borrows no mask to hide its natural deformity.—We cannot act with too much circumspection. All vice is progressive—every faulty indulgence exposes to farther deviations; and the woman who, by a levity of behaviour, excites improper wishes and expectations, is not only herself in a very dangerous situation, but is answerable for the blameable inclinations with which she inspires others.

Though innocence is often less careful to preserve appearances, than real guilt, yet to despise the loss of reputation, to be regardless of the effects of our example, or of any undue influence, frequently leads to the loss of virtue. An attention to reputation is sometimes the sole defence against a criminal indulgence—but I wish your conduct to be founded on more exalted and consistent motives.

My dear Clara, will you pardon the liberty I have taken?—My intention requires no apology. I love you so well as to wish to see you entirely arrived at that perfection to which you make such near approaches.—Be assured I shall rejoice when an union with my brother will give me a right to subscribe myself your sister, though that alliance cannot add to the regard with which

I am,

my dear Miss Woodford,

your most faithful friend,

CAROLINE HERBERT.

LETTER L.

To Mrs. Herbert.

I CANNOT be silent, my best of friends, lest you should suspect that I am offended by the dictates of the noblest friendship.

I have called your's, severe virtue; but, ah! most excellent of women, it was when my conduct degenerated from your principles.—You possess more than maternal tenderness, united with manly dignity of mind.—My whole soul is in your hands. Mould it as you please. I plead guilty to every charge, and trust to the clemency of my earthly benefactress, and to the mercy of my heavenly Judge.

Words are inadequate to express the esteem and love, with which

I am,

my dearest Madam,

your gratefully devoted

CLARA WOODFORD.

LETTER LI.

To Miss Herbert.

WILL you, my dear Miss Herbert, admit once more to your friendship, the poor wanderer from her duty, who has severely suffered for forsaking it?

Did you not observe my guilty attachment, and the horrid envy which possessed my heart?—O, my dear, I have been one of the most miserable of human beings, in consequence of having been one of the most faulty. That chearfulness, which pleased others, and was a proof of my own serenity, was entirely banished.

Who can be more wretched than she who condemns and detests herself, and who, with the loss of the most delightful consciousness, has also lost even the wish to become better?—This has been my deplorable case—but my heart is now at ease. I look back with horror on my criminal passion, and indulge none now of which I have reason to be ashamed.

I begin to resume my gaiety, but I have bidden a final adieu to levity. Conquests and flattery appear no longer desirable.—I have been a giddy and a guilty creature. No softenings, child, I am now above them. It is this detestable varnish which conceals the real deformity of vice.

How foolish have I been in ridiculing a love founded on esteem, and sanctified by every religious and moral tie. A love, such as we ought to endeavour to deserve, as a sanction which only can form the highest temporal happiness.

You have often, from pure humility, and a too high opinion of my personal attractions, told me you never expected to engage the serious attentions of any man, whilst I continued unmarried. How unjust to you, and how unworthy of themselves was the preference given to me by superficial observers!—For the future I will not desire to excel

"In a set of features and complection, but in

"Inward greatness, unaffected wisdom,

"And sanctity of manners."

May Mrs. Herbert's "soul shine out in every thing I act or speak."—I assure you, my dear, I have had some trials of my resolution, but it remains unshaken. Two admirers with very different qualifications have declared their wishes to live with me, or their inclination to die for me.

One of them is Sir Henry Farsfield, with an estate of £5000. a year; the other, a Captain Westley, with as fine a face and person as ever captivated a female heart. Mine however has not felt one palpitation, nor has my vanity protracted the siege. I gave them an absolute negative on their declaration, and have since insisted on their visiting me no more.

Would you believe it, my dear?—The creatures are absolutely, positively, both of them alive, eat, drink, and dress, as well as ever: and I hear that the Captain had power even to dance last night at a private ball.—O these deceitful men! Their tragic rant is a mere farce—their life a masquerade.

Seriously, my dear Lucy, I do not wish them to be uneasy, but I want them to be sincere. Vain expectation! but I have no more to say to them. Mr. Berkeley is an exception, and he cannot wish me to be more susceptible than I am of his merit. How happy for me that my vanity, folly, and ignorance, of my heart, did not alienate his from me. Avaunt, for ever, the spirit of coquetry! May I act from the influence of rational love, and sincere friendship, and be equal to the performance of every duty of life.

Continue to me your affection, my dear, for it is essential to the happiness of

your sincerely faithful,

CLARA WOODFORD.

LETTER LII.

To Miss Woodford.

COULD you, my beloved friend, entertain a single apprehension of your being less dear to me than ever? I own I thought you had encouraged, insensibly encouraged, a dangerous passion, and I pitied you for the delusion: but you have now resumed your former self; your gaiety is returned, and your sportive innocence enlivens and delights as usual.

Your account of your lovers made me smile, but your just sense of Mr. Berkeley's merit renders me happy. Be assured, my sweet friend, you are inexpressibly dear to my sister, and to your ever faithful

LUCIA HERBERT.

LETTER LIII.

To Mrs. Berkeley.

Dear Madam,

WE have had an unexpected meeting with Mrs. Fenning at a visit we made since my last letter.—We had passed a very agreeable hour, when she was announced.

As soon as she had cast her eyes on Mrs. Herbert, disdain took possession of all her features. I saw she sate studying to make some ill-natured observations, and I dreaded their effect upon my sister. The conversation turned upon plays. Amongst the rest, the Jealous Wife came under our inspection. Mrs. Fenning launched forth. "It is an odious character," exclaimed she, "and I always delight in seeing it rendered ridiculous. But the secure wife, who thinks her charms can never be slighted, is still more absurd. This is an unusual character however, for experience has convinced most women of their frail dependence on mankind; but I do know some ladies who expect their husbands should be entirely devoted to them, and centre their delights in domestic duties.

As to myself, I neither expect nor desire constancy from Mr. Fenning. I have had my share of his admiration; let others take their turn. I shall not be destitute of admirers. I would by all means have him please himself.—Let my visionary acquaintance, Mrs. Robertson, and other dove-like females, profess and expect constancy. I know human nature better. I do not ask for miracles in my favour."

My brother sate in visible confusion during this conversation. How delightful, how animating, is the consciousness of innocence! He, who used to enliven every society, and whose exalted sentiments convinced others of their own deficiencies, was now silent, self-condemned, and unhappy.

My sister saw, and shared his uneasiness. Mrs. Fenning's cruel attempt to occasion distress, would have had too much the appearance of a triumph, if it had remained unanswered. My sister, I believe, thought so too: "if I may judge of Mrs. Robertson by myself," said she, "it is not vanity, but esteem, which excites her confidence in her husband. She endeavours to act as the conviction of her judgment and her heart tell her she ought to act, and she relies on the fidelity it is the study of her life to deserve from her husband. Her serenity is then the result of principle."

Mrs. Fenning yawned affectedly.

More company entering, other subjects were introduced. She tried to coquet with my brother, but he was inaccessible to all her attacks, and I never saw him more thoughtful.—She then planted her battery against Mr. Millner, a young and very agreeable gentleman, but she met with another unexpected repulse. This was so mortifying that she soon made her exit, and the scene changed.

The remainder of the evening was spent in a very agreeable manner: my sister was all herself. She banished every painful thought, and appeared so unaffectedly chearful, that my brother's melancholy gave place to a delightful serenity, which displayed itself in his looks and conversation. My sister's eyes sparkled with uncommon lustre on observing this alteration; her whole person was animated, her conversation was enlivened by the desire of pleasing her husband, who gazed on her with the tenderest admiration.

Mr. Millner observed to him, that, for chearfulness without levity, prudence without censoriousness, and delicacy free from prudery, he never saw Mrs. Herbert's equal.—My brother enjoyed her praises, yet sighed, no doubt from a painful recollection, while she, elevated by his apparent approbation, never appeared more amiable and happy.

Surely my brother will rise superior to every allurement that alienates him from this excellent woman.—How can he be sensible to her unequalled merit?—Ah! madam, I wrong him—he is not insensible—he feels her value.—May he soon restore to her the happiness of which he has deprived her!—You will then restore him to your esteem and maternal regards, and he will be as dear as ever to the heart of

your grateful and affectionate,

LUCIA HERBERT.

LETTER LIV.

To Lord Wilton.

INDEED, my Lord, I believed myself to be equal to any task you could have assigned me, but, I find, we both over-rated my abilities.

I had read instances of consummate virtue, of unconquerable chastity, and of invulnerable fidelity; but I considered them as romance, and expected not to meet with any such real character. Your Lordship, in your description of Mrs. Herbert, seemed to have formed a mere creature of the imagination. I felt a pleasure in the expectation of tracing imperfections in the mind and person of this idolized fair one; and my vanity received gratification from her imagined deficiencies.

I introduced myself to Mrs. Herbert, as a young lady, an acquaintance of Mrs. Bennet, who wanted to solicit her advice in a matter of the utmost consequence. I had attired myself in all the elegance of a morning undress. I was presently admitted.

I entered Mrs. Herbert's dressing-room with a confidence which was soon repressed. Never did I see a more beautiful face, a more elegant form! What benign dignity shone in her fine eyes! Her dress bespoke the purity of her mind.—Nature was ornamented, not disguised.— What an inexpressibly-engaging manner!

Though prejudiced against her by your Lordship's warm encomiums, which I thought injurious to myself, yet I found the graces of her appearance and address irresistible.—I felt abashed—I blushed from conscious guilt. Her cheek seemed to be flushed with apprehension of my design. She enquired what had procured her the honour of this visit. My confusion rather befriended me.—My blushes, my hesitation were indications of my sufferings.

She heard the tale of my distresses with the tenderest sympathy.— She wept for me, but, when I mentioned the name of Mr. Herbert, she felt for him and for herself. An universal agitation affected her frame.—The colour forsook her lips and cheeks.—She raised her eyes for a moment to mine, as if to read my thoughts, then, fearful of tracing too much, she looked down with dejection.

I accused Mr. Herbert of having been the corrupter of my innocence; of having been long acquainted with me, and of having taken advantage of my distresses, to involve me in guilt.

Her cheek was instantly suffused with the deepest glow: her eyes sparkled with indignation.—She interrupted me.—"Miss Marston," said she, with an air of dignity, "you attempt to deceive me.—I am too well acquainted with Mr. Herbert's principles and disposition, to suspect him of villainy. He is incapable of being a seducer; he never was guilty of deliberate error, nor ever persisted in irregularity. His heart is fraught with so much benevolence, that I am convinced he never could be the instrument of increasing distress by guilt."

Her words, her manner, commanded respect and inspired awe. I never felt such reverence for any created being.—I was speechless. I dared not to re-assert what she had so positively refused to believe.

She saw my confusion;—the tears involuntarily gushed from my eyes.—"I pity you, with my whole soul," said she, "you have not injured me, but yourself. Confess your intended deception:—tell me your real distresses, and, if it be in my power to remove, or relieve them, depend on my assistance. Your manner has exculpated Mr. Herbert," pursued she, with some emotion.

What would I that moment have given, to have enjoyed so delightful a consciousness as she possessed! My mind was agitated. My wishes pleaded for the promotion of her happiness, but your threats alarmed my fears. I owned that I had been guilty of falsehood; that I had never seen Mr. Herbert more than once, but I solemnly assured her, though with deep contrition, that we had both been faulty.—She sighed—she lifted her eyes to heaven—she was silent.

After several minutes' pause, she resumed: "I am still convinced that Mr. Herbert never committed a premeditated error. Were circumstances known, I make no doubt they would greatly extenuate his fault.—Whoever was most to blame, may the penitence of both offenders secure forgiveness at the throne of mercy!"

She stopped—I could not speak—and she continued, "Gracious Heaven! what frail beings are we without thy aid!—This best of men has been permitted to decline from duty—may the sense of this deviation, become his future security by increasing his dependence on thee!"

Then turning to me, "Believe me," added she, with an energy dictated by benevolence, "I feel for you more than for myself. I have resources from conscious innocence—but it is in the Almighty alone I put my trust, or I am nothing.—You are certainly in distress; you could not come merely with a design of rendering me unhappy. Alas! it is only vice which can make us completely miserable—You have been guilty, perhaps you are still supported by the wages of iniquity. Tell me how I can serve and save you."—She took out her purse and put it into my hand.—"Accept of this trifle till I can be more extensively useful."

I was penetrated by her words and manner. I threw myself at her feet.—I promised to be implicitly guided by her advice; but I chose rather to write than to speak my shame.

And now, my Lord, what is the result? For you I abandoned friends and innocence! To you I gave myself, and my little fortune.— Forsaken by you, or considered merely as the vile instrument of promoting with others your lawless pleasures, I seemed to have lost all relish for virtue; but Mrs. Herbert has recalled my wandering inclinations, and I have now no wish but to return to my friends, and to endeavour to make my peace with Heaven.

I will never see you more. I only ask you to restore me to my little fortune. I hope I have yet a brother, who may be prevailed on to own, and receive me, if not entirely destitute: but, if you refuse to return me this poor pittance, I will throw myself on Mrs. Herbert's mercy, disclose to her every particular of our guilt, and leave it to her to determine the fate of the unhappy

SARAH MARSTON.

LETTER LV.

To Mrs. Herbert.

HOW completely happy, my dearest sister, should I be, if your merits were rewarded; but I dare not on this subject impart to you the dictates of my heart.

My reception from Miss Woodford has gratified my wishes. A soft, tender confusion on my entrance, rendered her appearance inexpressibly engaging. She has even condescended to acknowledge her caprice to me, and an undue sensibility of another's merit. Generous excellence! How has she exalted herself by what she calls a humiliating confession! I never before was so happy.

She tells me, the spirit of coquetry is entirely evaporated, and she convinces me, by her conduct, of the truth of her assertion. Every advantage of wealth, every charm of person has been tendered to her acceptance, and she has rejected them for my sake.—"And for my own, Mr. Berkeley," she adds, "for these are not the materials for husbands. The texture of their attachment is too slight for lasting wear, and as to money, you know Mr. Selden offered me my weight in gold, but I did not like the superabundance of lead in his own composition."

I must repeat that this amiable woman makes me the happiest of men.—Then she talks of you with such raptures, yet with so much judgment—no exaggeration—my heart expands with delight and love. Truly I can say with Jaffier:

"O woman! lovely woman! Nature made you
To temper man; we had been brutes without you;
Angels are painted fair to look like you;
There's in you all that we believe of heaven,
Amazing brightness, purity, and truth,
Eternal joy, and everlasting love."
And as truly subscribe myself

The Wife; or, Caroline Herbert

your ever affectionate brother

and faithful friend,

HENRY BERKELEY.

LETTER LVI.

To Henry Berkeley, Esq.

My dear Berkeley,

MY heart overflows with gratitude and thankfulness.—I have been enabled to discharge a duty. Ah! how many have been my omissions! how accumulated my transgressions!

You know Brumpton.—He formed a design on the fortune and person of a rich and beautiful heiress. She has a romantic turn, on which he built his hopes, and, with the assistance of a mercenary chambermaid, had very nearly completed his plan of operations. He solicited me to be the lady's father on the occasion.

I blushed then, Berkeley, and I still feel a conscious shame, and regret, on the reflection, that I have long been duped by a fellow void of humanity. With what arrogance and insensibility did he convince me that the fortune only was the object of his attachment. And then, degrading thought! he would not have dared to have made me the confidant of his intended enterprize had I not meanly degenerated into vice, and been fearful of detection.

But it would have been madness in me to have revenged myself on him for my own folly. I peremptorily told him I should take effectual means to prevent the prosecution of his purpose. He left me without making any answer.

Fearful of his undue influence, I immediately waited on the father, Brumpton having, when he requested my assistance, given me a direction. He appears to be one of the most amiable and respectable of men. His behaviour, his sentiments, all contributed to inspire me with this opinion. I am sure he is one of the tenderest, best of fathers.

He introduced me to his daughter—her appearance is truly engaging and interesting—her manners are soft and gentle. Mr. Forest, the father, gave me an opportunity of imparting to her the purport of my visit: her generous, unsuspecting, and prepossessed heart, unwillingly credited the deception; but at last I gained her entire belief; and her gratitude was as lively as her attachment had been sincere.

Her father oppressed me with acknowledgements, and wished to cultivate a friendship of which, alas! he thinks I am not unworthy.— I, who have wounded the peace of a whole amiable family, who have involved in distress the most excellent of women! And how miserable have I made myself. I, who was once the happiest of human beings!

Gracious Heaven!—I have erred against the conviction of my reason, and my conscience; against the law of my God, against my temporal and eternal happiness.

The beam of joy that enlivened my soul on having been the humble instrument of saving a fellow-creature from distress, has also invigorated my resolution of breaking those chains of vice which have long enthralled me.

"Aid me, blest providence."

At present, my dear Berkeley, I am unworthy of your esteem, and can only claim your pity.

Ever, ever your's,

CHARLES HERBERT.

LETTER LVII.

To Lord Wilton.

YOU were surprised, I make no doubt, my Lord, to find me not punctual to my appointment; but my scheme is utterly destroyed. That wretch Herbert threatens to acquaint Mr. Forest with my design. I have therefore left my lodgings privately, lest the intention of stealing an heiress should produce fatal consequences, and as my landlady may probably wish I had performed the usual ceremony of taking leave, I choose to lie perdu.

It is a lucky circumstance that I am ordered abroad so soon; but, my Lord, you must assist me.—Faith, I have very little of the ready, and travelling is expensive.—I must have a new suit. This is actually shabby. Your wardrobe is well filled.

Perhaps you will admire my calmness in supporting the loss of the lady.—I wish the lady had been the greatest loss. I should then have been quite a hero. The attendance, submission, and the thousand sedulities Miss Forest expected, were intolerable fatigues.—The attraction of fortune was indeed powerful. I was indefatigable. My dress and address were irresistible.

I wish you would make an attack on Herbert's wife.—You are very tedious in preparation. Surely you have not altered your purpose?—I must be revenged on him.—Be you my instrument—but I beg your pardon—you will disdain that office. Well then, let love to Mrs. Herbert, and hatred to her husband, as your unworthy rival, animate you.

I must leave town in a few days. Rejoice me before I go with an account of your success. It will be some consolation for the disappointment Herbert has occasioned me, as I know his happiness depends on his wife's fidelity.

Remember, my Lord, the deplorable consequences of an empty purse, and dispatch to me some relief. I am at — — — which is no very creditable place for your Lordship's reception. If you cannot come, send by a porter, that there may be no discovery; but, if the cordial can be administered with your own hand, it will have the most salutary effect on

your affectionate,

RICHARD BRUMPTON.

LETTER LVIII.

To Richard Brumpton, Esq.

So your scheme is entirely destroyed.—Poor Captain!—your purse is empty, and your dress shabby.—What a complication of distresses!—I cannot assist you with money, Dick, positively I cannot; for I have been stripped of every farthing this morning at White's.—I may perhaps send you a suit by and by,—I cannot see you this afternoon; my time is too precious.

Prithee, Dick, what sort of girl is thy Henrietta?—Is she handsome?—Will she repay the trouble of a pursuit?—The loss of the finest woman in the world would not affect you. It is only your vanity which seeks gratification.

Leave Herbert to me.—I do take upon me amply to revenge your cause.—I hope by artifice and rhetoric, to lull his wife to a forgetfulness of her honour. A fine woman neglected by her husband, is in a dangerous situation.—I am charmed with Mrs. Herbert, but I cannot slight every other woman to gratify this inclination.

I have not lost time with the husband, for I have tolerably fleeced his pockets, and seduced him from his happiness and duty.—You know it was for his wife's sake, I renewed my acquaintance with him; yet, wonderful effect, her majestic virtue has inspired me with so much awe, I have never dared to utter the remotest hint of love.

As to Sally Marston, would you believe it? the girl is squeamish.— She is so charmed with Mrs. Herbert, that she is eager to begin a reformation plan.—She chooses to take herself entirely out of my knowledge.—A little simpleton! I never wish to see her again; yet she has not a corrupt heart.—She was really unwilling to undertake the deception on Herbert, and was shocked on reflection.

I was a fool to trust her with Mrs. Herbert, yet, I hope, no harm is done. She has imparted to her his infidelity. That must have laid a foundation for me to build upon.

Sally wants me to refund, truly; I had £300. of her, but every sixpence has been long since gone; yet I did promise her, she should be repaid, if she entangled Herbert. She waits my answer, or she may discover all to Mrs. Herbert.—I will make one attempt,—if I fail, I must, by Sally's means, engage in some other trial.

This day, I hear, Herbert and his sister are to dine abroad. Berkeley and Miss Woodford are in the country.—Mrs. Herbert's little boy being somewhat indisposed, the mother's tenderness keeps her at home. I will manage, if possible, to infuse suspicions into her mind, which may facilitate my purpose. You shall know the result, if I have time from happier engagements to visit you. Adieu! your's,

WILTON.

LETTER LIX.

To Charles Herbert, Esq.

Dear Sir,

THE obligation you have conferred on me, in rescuing my only child from destruction, excited in my breast, sentiments of the most perfect gratitude and esteem. Your appearance was sufficient to inspire regard.

I could not help wishing for a more intimate acquaintance; but, as I learned from your own information that you were married, I was prompted by parental caution and tenderness, to enquire whether the character of your lady, in the opinion of the world, corresponded with the picture your love had painted.

Mrs. Herbert, the whole town proclaims, is a model of female perfection. Not even envy dares to vent a whisper to her prejudice.— Was it possible for the insinuating seducer to withdraw an husband's affection from such a wife?—And after she had blessed him with a sweet pledge of love?—Pardon me, if the incredulity excited by my esteem, was constrained to yield to the force of repeated information.

It is the advice of an excellent writer, "Not to believe all we hear, nor officiously to report all we believe." I was influenced by this precept.—I thought him, who had been the protector of innocence, incapable of betraying it to misery; especially where obligations claimed a right to the most constant affection.—I do not believe all I heard, but I have too much reason to be convinced every report is not without foundation.

You will think perhaps that I make an improper use of an acquaintance so lately begun, and from which I have derived such considerable advantage. You may censure me for officious zeal in attempting to dictate, where I am neither authorised by alliance, nor supported by intimacy.—But is not friendship a sufficient plea? Should not gratitude strongly incite us to save our benefactor from destruction? Do not social and religious ties prompt us to redress and prevent the misfortunes of our fellow creatures?

Mr. Herbert's heart feels the force of every generous emotion, though its effects have been for a time suspended where they should have been most powerfully exerted.—O let me intreat you to be influenced by the pleadings of your own heart, by conscience, by religion!

Think not that age has rendered me forgetful of the pleasure of youth. Chearfulness and content have always attended me. Heaven be praised, I enjoy them unmixed, because I have not to reflect on capital errors.—This assertion, if I know myself, is not the result of spiritual pride, but an effusion of humble gratitude. Far be it from me to conclude that I should have been victorious in trials where others have failed.—I mean only to recommend the armour of Christianity, which is alone impenetrable.

I attribute my serenity more to an uncommon care exerted by the best of parents in my education, and to the protection, the solicited protection of Heaven, than to my own strength of resolution.

Be assured that happiness does not consist in the indulgence, but restraint of unlawful inclinations, and that it is much easier to prevent the rise of passions, than to subdue them.

You are young, and perhaps unacquainted with mankind.—Early attached to a woman, worthy of the most exalted regard, your heart dilated with joy.—Truth, generosity, frankness, and delicacy, actuated every part of her conduct. From her, you judged of the world in general; and because she possessed the reality of virtue, you suspected not that any one could be satisfied merely with its appearance. And that a person dignified by truth, distinguished by fortune, and favoured by nature, could be capable of descending to the meanness of vice, was a suspicion your generous breast would not entertain.

By the unsuspecting goodness of your heart, you were first ensnared.

But remember, my dear sir, that true friendship can only be founded in virtue.—Be not influenced by bad example and ill-judged ridicule, to neglect the practice of essential duties!

Ah! do not defer to the winter of life, the extirpation of those weeds of vice, which, if suffered to take root, will over-run the soil, and obstruct the growth of every salutary plant.—Youth and health are the seasons for cultivating mental improvement; and how mean a sacrifice do we offer to God, when we delay it till we can no longer continue the votaries of pleasures!

How deplorable is their situation, who have stifled the workings of conscience, and lost the power of reflection!—How soon must they awake from a dream of sensuality, to all the horrors of a dreadful eternity.

You, sir, who possess every blessing, which reason can request or Heaven bestow, want only to be convinced of your happiness to secure the enjoyment of it.—You are united, by the most solemn ties, to a woman, whose merit alone should be esteemed sufficient to entitle her to the undivided possession of your heart.

Our divine law-giver has not only by his presence, sanctified the ceremonial of marriage, but, by a positive declaration, has enforced the duty of a strict observance of the connubial vow. "What God hath joined together, let not man put asunder."

Marriage is the state most agreeable to reason, and conformable to the dictates of morality.—A state, instituted by the divine author of our nature, to soften the asperities, and heighten the blessings of life.—Beware how you obstinately pervert the gracious purpose, and be assured, you cannot, with impunity, continue to violate those sacred vows which are registered in Heaven.

I have not mentioned the breach of that duty, the observance of which every man owes to himself, as well as to the community of which he is a member.—Can you reconcile the duties of a man and a Christian, with the commission of adultery, and an inattention to religious obligations?—Can any sensual pleasures compensate for the loss of innocence?—Impossible! On the contrary, experience evinces, that they are attended by disquietude, and succeeded by remorse.—For surely, when calm reflection takes place of insinuating passion, you must condemn yourself, and confess, there is no temporal happiness equal to that which results from the testimony of a good conscience; no hope so delightful, so invigorating, as that of receiving the plaudit of divine approbation.

In the female sex, reputation once lost, is scarcely ever to be regained; and though, from custom, and the degeneracy of mankind, unchastity is not considered as an heinous crime in ours, yet with the Almighty there is no distinction, and he will as severely punish the one as the other.

I hope you, sir, cannot be abandoned to guilt.—But if the considerations of duty, and futurity, are too weak to reclaim you from a habit of vice, let the fear of present misery deter you from an erroneous pursuit of happiness. Tremble, lest a perseverance in error, should estrange from you the affections of a wife, in whom all the perfections of her sex are centered.—Does her constant, her delicate regard, her submissive resignation to your will, her sedulous attention to please, appear less amiable, because they are the effects of duty, as well as the result of tender affection? This consideration should heighten your esteem and tenderness; for love, when under the guidance of virtue and religion, will subsist when time shall be lost in eternity!

From you, sir, I expect the most exalted triumph; the triumph of true honour over false shame.—A mind once fully impressed with a sense of duty, will soon, I hope, be enabled to recover its native dignity.

Were I writing to a man of the world, I should apologize for assuming a style, which would be deemed preceptive and dictatorial, but I have rated you by a higher standard, and, in addressing you, I have considered only the duty I owe to God, the cause of truth and virtue, and the best interests of a fellow creature and benefactor.

Believe me ever your grateful

servant and sincere friend,

ROBERT FOREST.

P.S. I find Brumpton embarks immediately for Jamaica. My daughter therefore is no longer obliged to shelter herself in retirement.

LETTER LX.

To Richard Brumpton, Esq.

I HAVE scarcely power to write; rage and disappointment tear my heart!—Yet I must disclose, or madness will ensue.—Prithee, let me have none of your nonsensical observations:—it is to avoid them, and your importunities, I determine not to see you.—I am unfit for conversation—I could do some horrid act, and leave my country for ever.—But I must begin.

I went to Herbert's house soon after his sister and he had left it. I was apprehensive Mrs. Herbert would refuse me admittance, but most fortunately, as I then thought it, she crossed the hall, when the servant opened the door. As I bowed to her, she could not avoid speaking; yet she immediately told me, Mr. Herbert was not at home. I hastily answered, "I would then beg a few moment's conference with her."—As I made this request before the servant, she could not refuse the grant of it, but I saw, by her looks, how much her heart disdained me.

When we entered the drawing-room, she coolly asked if I had any particular business with Mr. Herbert.—"No, madam," replied I, "nothing of importance—to say the truth, I rather wished to find you alone, having somewhat to communicate that demands your private ear."

"Whatever you have to say to me, my Lord," answered she, "cannot be improper for my husband to know.—I receive no private intelligence."— "I heartily wish, madam" said I, "Mr. Herbert's conduct was equally meritorious.—But"—

She started up—"My Lord," cried she, with an air of contempt,— "the man who dares to speak unfavourably to me of my husband, I regard as my worst enemy."

She approached the door—I caught her hand, and drew her gently back.—"What do you mean, my Lord?" said she, struggling to free herself.—"You must not leave me, madam," returned I.—"How? must not," repeated the charming creature, her eyes sparkling with indignation.

"No, madam, permit me to detain you," said I—"I come, as a friend, to offer you my advice and my assistance. If my zeal is offensive, it is well meant.—You are too tame. Are you not a mother as well as a wife? Upbraid him with your wrongs; force from him a different conduct.—His deviations shall be kept secret from the world for your sake."

"I disdain the appearance of an obligation to you," interrupted she; "my husband I consider as my best friend and safest counsellor."—"That husband," resumed I, "has neglected you, has been unfaithful, but while he sees you are easy, and depends on your fidelity, he will persist in his present conduct.—I have known many wives successful by exciting their husband's apprehensions of losing them.—The means will be sanctified by the proposed end."

"Lord Wilton," said she, with an air that commanded respect, and awhile silenced every selfish passion, "you convince me that you have rather expressed your wishes, than communicated your knowledge. I am not to be deceived by your sophistry; would you advise me to live a falshood?"

Her whole soul spoke in every animated feature.—On my honour, Brumpton, mine was awed by the dignity of virtue. Never before was I so humbled! It was some time before I could rally my scattered faculties. I then mentioned her husband's obligations to her.

She again interrupted me.—"Mr. Herbert," said she, "would have acted the same in similar circumstances."—"Yet," answered I, "are not all your duties fulfilled? Are not all his, violated? Are you not constrained to abridge even the exercises of beneficence? He has distrest himself and you by his love of play and other extravagancies—I have assisted him. He is again greatly involved:—

he knows not, but by my assistance, how to extricate himself. I will cancel his every former obligation, I will remove his every present difficulty, and ask no higher favour than your smile of approbation, and freely, kindly-extended hand."

I threw myself on my knees before her, and offered to seize her repulsive hand. She gazed on me with an eye which penetrated my very soul. "Pecuniary debts," said she, "can only be discharged by pecuniary considerations. The smile of approbation and the hand of kindness, can only be extended to the sincere friend. Have you been such, Lord Wilton?"

By my soul, I trembled and turned pale as her eye met mine.

I was attempting to speak, when she continued, lifting up her fine eyes to Heaven, "Can there be such villainy in man?—Do not dare to imagine that I am the dupe of your vile insinuations.—Thou mean invader of the rights of an injured husband, thy artifice is too gross to impose on me!—To seduce the wife, the husband's character must be the sacrifice.—I despise thy cruel stratagem.—Mr. Herbert's merit rises to my delighted remembrance, and I am confirmed in the opinion of his excellence, by this farther conviction of thy depravity.—But to converse with thee is injurious to the dignity of affronted virtue.—May remorse awaken you to amendment, and may you never more attempt to corrupt innocence!"

She then hastily quitted the room.—With what elevation of sentiment did she triumph over me!—I was flying after her, when I met, in the next apartment, the happy husband.

He saw my confusion.—I knew I had injured him in intention. I wished to revenge on him my disappointment.—But, the deuce take him—the fellow would not fight.—He talked of duty, and honour, and—I know not what; a pretended fit of awakened conscience. A fool! his conscience should have restrained him from yielding to my insinuations.

Where was this bosom friend, when this wife was forsaken by him, and he joined me in pursuits, which he knew were contrary to his duty?—But the truth was, he feared to engage with me—so I left the house, disappointed both in love and revenge.

What could be done with such a woman? I had early tried the arts of flattery—but why do I call it flattery?—She is superior to all praise.—I followed her every where. I endeavoured to please, to be useful to her. A thousand little officious services have I rendered her, to which she returned only a cold politeness.—I was always of her opinion.—I praised no one else.—Never did any other woman ever treat me with such indifference.—Did you ever know these methods fail?—She has annihilated my whole system.—Had her guardian angel for one moment deserted his charge, had she in the least relaxed from her rigid watchfulness, I should have thought myself secure of a deliberate success.

But I can waste no more time on you. I must invent some new project, or, I believe, I shall entirely lose my senses.—I cannot bear a formal conclusion.—You know the characters of

your

WILTON.

LETTER LXI.

To Miss Herbert.

WHAT monstrous encroachers these men are, Lucy!—I had resolutely determined on absolute monarchy for several months to come, when this Berkeley, this usurper, invades my rights, tramples on my laws, wants me, truly! to delegate all my authority, and to render to him my oath of allegiance.—To acknowledge him as my supreme head, and to become a subject, instead of a sovereign. What a bashaw!

And must I vow "to love, to honour, and to obey, and to keep him not only for better, but for worse; not only in health, but in sickness; and this as long as we both shall live"? I am well read in the matrimonial service,—I have got it by heart, (as it is vulgarly exprest) and this man has certainly taken possession of my heart, or I should never promise to subscribe to these articles, which I believe I shall soon do with my whole heart and soul.

He has written to Mrs. Berkeley, and she has answered his letter* with her wishes joined to his.—Mrs. Bennet is teazing, and her husband provoking.—She is my only relation, she urges, and she cannot go to London.—And Mr. Bennet has no notion of such long courtships.—The parties, he says, have worn their love suit quite threadbare, before they make up their wedding garments.

Then Mr. Berkeley is so—what shall I call it?—so generously tender, that he has almost triumphed over all my resolves.—Yes, my dear friend, I believe I shall actually have entered upon the formidable estate of matrimony, before we meet again. It is however an honourable estate.

I shall promise nothing but what I will religiously endeavour to perform, as, I am convinced, what is enjoined, is no more than ought to be performed.—I have not yet however consented to fix a day, but every day of my life shall be devoted to Mr. Berkeley's happiness.

In witness whereof I set my hand and seal.

CLARA WOODFORD.

LETTER LXII.

To Miss Woodford.

MY sweet, lively friend! My heart sincerely congratulates you on your approaching happiness, and applauds you for your ingenuous confessions.

Mrs. Bennet has reason in her argument, yet my sister and I are unwilling to be from you at such a time; and for me to lose the office of bridesmaid, is it not mortifying?—But we shall expect you in town very soon after the ceremony, and be impatient till you arrive.

My brother has been more at home than usual; he is more than ever attentive to my sister. He gazes on her "till the big tear stands trembling in his eye."—Surely their fate is near its crisis!—Dear, dear creatures, my heart bleeds for both! May all happiness attend you, my sweet friend, prays

your ever affectionate,

LUCIA HERBERT.

LETTER LXIII.

To Henry Berkeley, Esq.

MY brother! my friend! I now dare call you by that expressive name. My whole soul is overwhelmed with the deepest remorse, and yet expanded with the most lively gratitude.—Read the enclosed letter.* The God, whom this good man and my Caroline have always served, is able to deliver me."

Lord Wilton is a villain. He has attempted to poison my Caroline's mind, and to make to himself an interest in her affections.—I met him in my house. Never shall I forget the conscious rage and guilt that flashed in his eyes, nor the mingled terror with which he viewed me. He endeavoured to pass me. I asked him to explain his behaviour.—"My Lord! you leave not the house till you have satisfied my enquiry.—Speak, lest I violate the laws of hospitality." My soul was in tumults.

He stammered—"Come, prithee Herbert, what reason have you for anger? Do you think, because you have no eyes to admire the most lovely of women, that others must be blind to her beauty? Have you a right to insult me? You, who have most cruelly injured her!"

"Ah! wretch," said I, "did you not estrange me from my duty, and withdraw my person, you cannot say my heart, from the most excellent of women?"

This parley encouraged him to answer readily,—"Had you been settled in your principles, my insinuations had not prevailed."

Though from the mouth of an enemy, I could not be deaf to the voice of truth.—What a caution would this example afford to the unsteady mind! I became the object of his contempt to whom I had sacrificed my duty!

I stood abashed on the recollection of my design.—Passion had almost hurried me into the commission of another crime.—My wife and child rendered life desirable that I might discharge the debt I owed to them. I dared not rush to meet death, and leave unperformed the duties of life.—I considered that I might live to be happy, and to make others happy, and that my misery commenced with my deviation from duty.

My continued silence, and an appearance of irresolution, inspired my treacherous adversary with some sparks of courage.—"Come, sir," said he, "I will follow where you please. I do not mean to parley."

"No," answered I,—"I have reflected on my own conduct, which appears to be so blameable, I dare not defend it.—My deviations have indeed more cruelly wounded my wife than even your baseness. It shall be the study of my life to make all the atonement in my power. Be it your's to correct your vicious inclinations.—Begone! I forgive you—I seek no revenge.—You have defended my life—I will not attempt your's.—Let me never see you more, lest I forget my resolution and chastise you for a villain.—In a just cause, my sword shall always be readily exerted, but I dare not venture myself, nor would I send you into the presence of offended omnipotence."

My behaviour, the place, and the sight of some of the servants at a little distance, animated him so much that he cried,—"You have no obligations to me—I saved not your life—it never was in real danger—I always meant to betray you.—And are you really afraid?—Poor Herbert!"

I frowned indignant.—He changed colour, and only added, "Well then, to part friends, it is best to leave you abruptly"—and instantly quitted the house.

How my heart rejoiced in my escape from farther guilt!—I retired to my study to indulge reflection, for I was too much discomposed to appear before my wife.

O! Berkeley, though my heart has been bewildered in the labyrinth of vice, it never ceased its wishes to regain the path of virtue.—Difficulty weakened my endeavour.—A false friend deceived me with the shadow of honour.

Ah! if my Caroline will accept a sincere penitent, her forgiveness, and restored affection will excite my hopes of the divine pardon, and, I humbly trust, secure my reformation.—But can she forgive me?—Shall I solicit Mr. Forest to plead for me?—No, I will owe all to her own goodness and affection: to that excellence, which, like Heaven, will receive and accept the contrite offender.

But I must attend Mr. Forest. My soul is humbled by a deep sense of guilt. I dread to appear before him, but I will conquer all false shame, and confess all my obliquities. I will write again on my return from this good man.—Adieu! till then.

I am

ever most cordially your's

CHARLES HERBERT.

LETTER LXIV.

To Henry Berkeley, Esq.

Dear Brother,

I FOUND this sincere friend at home, and alone. He received me with the utmost benignity; and after the usual civilities, seeing me in apparent confusion:

"Mr. Herbert," said he, "the motive which induced me to write, acquits me to myself of impertinent zeal, and, I hope, will plead my apology with you. There is an ingenuous concern expressed in your countenance, which convinces me I did not err in my opinion of the goodness of your heart.—You will become all I wish you."

The tears gushed from his eyes as he endeavoured to say more. He grasped my hand with all the warmth of gratified benevolence. It was some time before I was enough composed to reply, "O! my father—my heart has long struggled between the conviction of duty, and the influence of error.—What have I suffered since my deviation! I supplicated for divine assistance, determined never more to tread the slippery paths of vice; but alas! whilst I prayed to be delivered from temptation, I rashly ventured into its mazes.— Your advice strengthens my every good purpose. Continue to me that friendship you have so generously exerted—I will study to deserve it."

Softened by his tender sympathy, and truly affected with a sense of past errors, I was constrained to be silent. "These tears," said Mr. Forest, "flow from a contrite heart, and will doubtless be accepted by the Almighty.

"But let me caution you against a depression of spirit, hardly less fatal to the practice of religion, than the sallies of passion.—The melancholy of enthusiasm, and the rigours of superstition, but ill supply the deficiency of those virtues they mean to represent.

Religion diffuses an unclouded cheerfulness over the aspect, and beams forth in the perpetual sunshine of benevolence.

"Let the examples in holy Scripture of pardon to offenders, revive your hopes, and animate your practice. These examples, whilst they afford encouragement to true penitents, should soften the severity of virtue, and teach her professed votaries to be merciful, even as our Father which is in heaven, is merciful."

I could not refrain from interrupting the venerable man, by catching his hand, and exclaiming, whilst I gave it a strenuous pressure,— "Proceed, dear sir, and instruct me how to practise those duties in which you are so well established."

"I was afraid," he answered, with a glow of benevolence, "you would have thought my advice tedious; but I beg your pardon. There are subjects, on which to trifle is a proof of folly; and duties, which to neglect, is the height of madness. Believe me, sir, a time will come when those who have squandered happiness in pursuit of pleasure, will vainly wish to recall the precious hours they have mispent.—A state of health is the proper season for repentance."

"What thanks," cried I, "what gratitude I owe you! But alas! will not the knowledge of one sad stain of guilt tincture the whole of an otherwise unblemished life?—Will not common frailties be deemed the result of a vicious inclination?"

"With the truly good and candid," answered Mr. Forest, "repentance being succeeded by perseverance in duty, will not only be a proof of sincerity, but secure a re-establishment of reputation. The good opinion of the world ought not to be disregarded, though it does not constitute our real merit; but let a nobler incitement animate your practice, and suffer not the insinuations of malice to ruffle your tranquillity, nor disturb your laudable pursuits.—Remember there is, there can be no safety but in religion.

"Suffer neither the dread of contempt, nor the prevalence of bad example to render you ashamed of shewing an invariable esteem and affection for your wife. I am far from recommending that childish and troublesome fondness, which makes the spectators uneasy, and the parties ridiculous, but there is a conspicuous, manly tenderness, an exalted friendship, which feels and imparts delight, and reflects equal honour on those who pay, and those who receive it.

"Never be influenced by the modish custom of appearing disgusted with diversions, because your wife is present.—You pay an ill compliment to your own judgment, when you are guilty of inattention to her. The pursuit of different amusements dissipates the affection; and though absence is sometimes unavoidable, true love will never find it necessary to its own preservation. I grant that the joy of meeting calls forth all the tenderness of susceptible hearts; but they who wish to prove the satisfaction by losing awhile the object who is to inspire it, are conscious there is a coolness in their affection which requires particular circumstances to exalt it to a degree worthy of the name of love."

"My reason and my heart," replied I, "assent to the truth of your opinion. Happy is he who finds a gentle monitor to advise, and a bright example of Christian virtue, to animate him to the discharge of his duty!—Most happy he who never erred! The world's contempt, and distressful circumstances, may plunge many into repeated acts of guilt, whom a more favourable situation, and milder treatment, might have reclaimed."

"You are certainly in the right," rejoined Mr. Forest, "and I wish the abhorrence generally expressed against vice, was the effect of a settled habit of virtue; but alas! were it so, the truly penitent would be received into the number of the virtuous, with as much joy, as the real criminal was expelled from their society with pity and regret. 'The Deity (say some) is the only true judge of sincere repentance. Man is frequently deceived by appearances—They who have once been frail, may naturally be suspected of being again endangered by the force of temptation, and therefore ought not to be trusted.'

"Are these sentiments the dictates of humanity? Shall the tormenting passions of suspicion and distrust be permitted to banish from the breast that charity which is the essence of the Christian religion?— Should the same temptations solicit, where is the bold champion of virtue, who dares engage the attacks of vice with a certainty of conquest?—How often has presumption suffered, when it has *sought* occasions of triumph?

"Is there any man who, in judging another, can on an impartial retrospect, acquit himself of having never swerved from his duty? When he finds himself fallible (and who is impeccable?) he will drop a tear of pity for his weak brother, and implore the Almighty's forgiveness for *him*, as he hopes forgiveness of his own offences.— Forgiveness of injuries if a ruling principle of Christianity— Universal benevolence is true charity. We may be circumscribed by providence in our ability to distribute alms, but the social feelings of the heart, may extend towards all human kind.

"It afflicts me, Mr. Herbert," continued this excellent man, "when I find the doctrines of Christianity contemned and disregarded, because they are promulgated by those who appear to be actuated by motives of temporal interest to defend them. I am afraid it will always be the case, that where worldly advantages are annexed to the profession of teaching duty, the professors will be deemed by some to be hypocritical and interested, and their instructions considered by others as unmeaning declamations.—Perfection is expected from a clergyman, when, alas! the same passions incite, the same temptations solicit, the same frail creature is overcome! yet it is certain that men of our profession, from the natural tendency of their studies, have better opportunities than others, of improvement; and from persons of superior abilities, 'to whom much has been given, from them much will be required:' but whilst, on the one hand, the holy office is degraded into contempt, by an improper choice of its ministers; on the other, the generality of mankind will not be convinced a man chooses to devote himself to the church on spiritual, rather than temporal considerations.—If any persons are displeased with his doctrine, they will very strictly search into his life, view it with the jaundiced eye of prejudice, and be much more ready to magnify the mote in his eye, than to cast the beam from their own. It is likewise greatly to be lamented, that they who actually feel the true spirit of charity, are not able to practise what they teach;—that they can only breathe forth their prayers and wishes, and contribute their mite towards the assistance of their fellow creatures, without the power of bestowing *sufficient* relief.— Even where domestic claims forbid the exertion of public charity, want of ability will frequently be misconstrued into want of benevolence."

Every word this good man uttered increased my esteem and admiration. My heart glowed with the most tender sensations of gratitude.—I soon after took leave, intreating him to honour me with his friendship and acquaintance, and to permit me to introduce my Caroline to Miss Forest.

Adieu! my dear Berkeley.—I intended to have sought an interview with the best beloved of my heart, but I am not equal to it.—I must write—I tremble, and am a coward when I look up to her superlative excellence.—If she receive me to her favour, how inexpressibly happy, yet alas! how self-condemned will be

her ever devoted,

and your truly affectionate,

CHARLES HERBERT.

LETTER LXV.

To Mrs. Herbert.

IN what manner, dearest, most amiable, and excellent of women, shall I presume to address you, after my sad defection from you and duty?—Ah! my Caroline, how little did I once imagine I could have been capable of injuring you:—that even a thought could wander from the object of my plighted vows.

Fatally trusting to my own strength, and to my love for you, I resumed an acquaintance with a wretch, whose aim I am convinced, was to mislead me, and seduce you.—Your ever-wakeful dependence on Heaven, preserved you:—my self-confidence betrayed me.—Yet, dearest excellence, believe me whilst I assure you, my heart, my esteem, never wandered from you.

Vanity, false shame, the levity of the objects around me, contributed to my deviation; yet I avoided many occasions, by which the arch enemy meant to ensnare me.—Alas! even in my escapes I had cause for humiliation, for do not the laws of Christianity search out the thoughts, and prove the heart, and did not the necessity of flight determine mine to be culpable?

The dishonourable Peer, I am now certain, contrived a tale which engaged my sympathy.—He influenced the object who deceived me, and armed the ruffians who attacked me, that he might make himself appear to be the instrument of my defence. Best of women! Am I not an alien from your affections? have you not entirely banished me from your heart? Despair surrounds me at the thought; for if you abandon me, I must be forsaken by Heaven.

You once loved me, my Caroline.—Ah! how inestimable a proof did you give me of your affection. Why did I say a proof? Your whole life has been an invariable testimony of your love.

Alas! how many tears must I have caused you to shed!—yet lest I should be made unhappy by the knowledge of your sufferings, you endeavoured to wear the semblance of chearfulness. How painful must have been that task to the most ingenuous of human minds. And could that appearance lessen the sense of guilt to any other than an infatuated wretch?—My Caroline! I detest myself when I reflect on your sufferings.—I know you will not reproach me, but my whole future life must be marked with self-upbraidings.

I dared not to speak on this heart-affecting subject. I was convinced I could not have said all that my mind has long laboured with.—My Caroline! My Wife! O, will you re-admit to your love, your friendship, your confidence,

Your truly penitent and

ever faithful husband,

CHARLES HERBERT.

LETTER LXVI.

To Mr. Herbert.

IT is impossible for me, my dearest life, to describe the contrary emotions which assailed my heart on reading your letter.—Tender grief, joy, self-reproach, by turns agitated my mind.—But oh! my beloved Mr. Herbert, can you for a moment encourage a doubt of my affection and esteem?

I own, I *have* suffered.—I have been greatly distressed.—I knew not how to act.—Sometimes I intended gently to insinuate my apprehensions and wishes.—Then I feared to offend, or wound you.—I dreaded lest I should seem to arrogate to myself, a supposed superiority.—I saw you thoughtful and disquieted.—I hoped the workings of your mind would have a happy effect on your conduct, and I wished to see you re-instated in every duty, by the force of your own Christian principles.—My dearest husband! never would I have trusted my present and future happiness to any but a man of principle. The reformation of a libertine, and an infidel, was a task of too Ethiopian a dye for me to attempt, and such a connexion is injurious to female delicacy.

I had long known your benevolent heart, and found it to have been invariably actuated by religious motives.—An acquaintance with a specious profligate, gay company, infectious examples awhile entangled that generous and unsuspecting heart; but with a noble exertion of principle, you burst the fetters of vice, and with the assistance of Heaven have obtained the triumph of virtue.

Do not, my beloved husband, my best of friends, do not indulge a desponding thought. Even your past errors will be converted into the means of your future security by a firmer reliance on Providence.

You feel the necessity of an unremitted dependence on Him, who alone is able to save; of constant and fervent supplications, united supplications at the throne of grace. We were formed in weakness, that we might *rely only on His strength.* Let us resume, let us never omit the noblest of family exercises.

I beg, I intreat, my dearest Mr. Herbert, that you will never more mention a subject which would give pain to both. Be assured, that my love and esteem, which were ever yours, are increased to the highest degree.

Come then, my best beloved! Let there be but one heart, one soul, to animate our actions, and oh! let every painful remembrance be banished from the breast of the most affectionate of husbands, as it shall be from the memory of

his ever-tenderly faithful wife,

CAROLINE HERBERT.

LETTER LXVII.

To Miss Herbert.

Honoured Madam,

MY poor old heart is almost broke.—My dear master is almost distracted.—I'll tell you the reason as well as I can.

He went this morning to Mr. Milton's.—I was to call him, and when I got there, I found him walking backwards and forwards about the room, like a madman. I begged to know what was the matter, but he could not tell me.—A man, who was with him, and who I found had been a servant of Lord Wilton's, told me, that his master went off this morning with an intention of going abroad, he did not know where, and that he knew he meant to surprise, and take Mrs. Herbert with him.

You know, Madam, my mistress and the child went an airing this morning, and he may very possibly have taken her away, yet the servant don't seem to be certain of any thing. He has been turned off, and he has heard my lord mention such a design.

For God's sake, Madam, come to us, for I am afraid my master should do himself a mischief.—O! that my mistress may be come home.—Dear, good Madam, come and save my master, and comfort the heart of

your old faithful and distressed servant,

JOHN STANLEY.

LETTER LXVIII.

To Mrs. Henry Berkeley.

INSTEAD of congratulating you on your marriage, ah! my dear friend, how must I alarm you!

What an interruption to your and our happiness!

Where, oh where is my angelic sister?—Mr. Bennet's servant calling to enquire after us, I am fearful he should drop a hint of our present uneasiness, which might be more alarming to you if possible, than particulars of the truth.

O my dear, we have some reason to fear that Lord Wilton has surprised, and carried off my sister, who went out this morning with the child, and is not yet returned. I expected my mantua-maker, or I should have attended her.

About three o'clock, a note was brought to me, from John Stanley. I inclose it—You may believe I flew immediately to my brother. I found him violently agitated. His looks were disordered. John Stanley was on his knees before him, the tears trickling down his aged cheeks.

As soon as my brother saw me, he started, ran to me, and clasping me to his breast, "O my sister," he cried, "I have lost my Caroline!—My God, what will become of me!"

The tenderest sympathy kept me awhile silent—at last, I joined my intreaties with those of the good old servant, that he would return home, and we would think of every means to recover my sister, if the misfortune was real.

The hope I encouraged, suspended his affliction. We came home, Mr. Milton with us, whom I intreated to accompany my brother to Sir

Henry Romney's for information. They were just gone as your servant called.

* * * * *

Good God! what various agitations. We lamented a fancied evil, and have now to deplore a real calamity.—My sister and the child have been overturned.—The coach brought them home about an hour since; the child very little bruised, but my sister in fits.—Dr. H—— is with her, and I think his looks betray her danger.

* * * * *

My brother is this moment returned, relieved from some fears, but distressed by others. Sir Henry solemnly protested that though Lord Wilton might lightly talk of such a project, he never seriously designed to attempt it; and to convince him, shewed him a letter from that nobleman, which affords some gleams of hope of his reformation.

My brother's anxiety is inexpressible.—Judge of it from his love and her merits.—Alas! it was on the eve of a reconciliation that this dreadful misfortune happened. This circumstance increases our regrets.

I slipt out of the room to give you this intelligence, as your servant says he must return this evening. I am shocked at the uneasy suspense I must occasion.—My heart is torn with apprehension.—O gracious God, spare her to us!—Come to town immediately.

Your's most truly,

LUCIA HERBERT.

LETTER LXIX.

To Charles Herbert, Esq.

I HAVE reason to believe, my dearest Mr. Herbert, that a few hours will consign me to immortality, and death has no terrors but the thoughts of a separation from you, my mother and my child, and our fraternal friends. There I own, resolution fails, and fortitude is shaken!

O best beloved of my soul, to lose you now, when we were more tenderly, and firmly united than ever.—Human nature knows not how to support the idea.—yet do not I intreat you, do not cherish a fruitless affliction for my death; but transfer to our child that tender love which is now my highest temporal blessing.

I am still dear to you;—I know I shall *ever* be very dear to you, but mourn not for the happy! I trust not in my own merits that I *shall* be happy.—If you would exalt even my heavenly felicity, O my best and dearest of earthly friends, it must be by becoming a partaker of it.—I still offer up my most fervent prayers for you!—The same Almighty Being, who has been my defence in trouble, will sustain you. When you arrive at the last awful moment, you will find with me that the recollection of virtuous and religious actions, and principles, affords the only pure delight.

When I think that I shall soon part from you, never to meet again in this world, and that most probably, I have given my mother and child a last embrace, conjugal, filial, and maternal love divide my soul!

My heart is too deeply affected, to express its emotions, but the struggle will soon be over!—I feel the efficacy of Christianity!—I acknowledge the gracious assistance of the Omnipotent!—Though unconscious of unintentional errors, it is a CHRISTIAN *hope* alone that supports me—The pains of dissolution are transient, and beyond this life, all is felicity!—Whilst I contemplate future bliss, methinks I already feel a Heaven in my breast!

Dearest of men! farewell! May our enlarged spirits meet again in an happy eternity!

CAROLINE HERBERT.

A Letter to Mrs. Berkeley, with some account of the sad accident, is omitted, as its contents are similar to those in Letter LXVIII.

LETTER LXX.

To Lord Wilton.

ALAS! my dear Lord, my revenge is still imperfect—What a mean wretch is this fellow!—I once declined turning my sword upon him, for reasons too tedious now to mention.

But hark ye, my Lord;—let me give you one piece of advice. Your seduction of the young lady, which you imagined to be a profound secret, is divulged to her father, who vows revenge for the injury.— Her death, with every horrid circumstance, is known to him. He is as violent in vengeance, as you are in your passions for the fair sex.

I wish you had satisfied your own inclination, and revenged my quarrel. Then you would have had an additional reason to have fled the kingdom—but it is now too late for farther attempts.—Your life is most certainly in danger. I had this intelligence from a person who knows nothing of our connexion, and I cannot doubt the truth of the report.

Come then, my Lord, let us embark together.—We can be as happy in another country, as in England. Change of climate need not produce any change of manners.—You may pursue your favourite amusements, and assist your old friend in a less expensive folly. Or to speak more *tenderly* and *poetically,*

> We'll still improve the talents we possess,
> *Your* study, pleasure, *mine,* a taste for dress.

Come, my Lord, support your usual gaiety.—You will not leave many friends behind you, and by being a friend to me, you will secure to yourself one in

RICHARD BRUMPTON.

LETTER LXXI.

To Richard Brumpton, Esq.

> Must I then leave thee, paradise?
> Thus leave
> Thee, native soil? This *happy town and court,*
> The haunt of *beauties*?

Is this the result of my projects?—To be driven from my native land?—Forced to seek asylum amongst strangers?—But to confess the truth, Brumpton, I must seek happiness, if I stay at home, for I never yet have found it.—Instead of procuring my own gratification by promoting the welfare of others, my whole life has been made a scene of wretchedness, by the indulgence of every vagrant inclination.

Herbert was entangled by my snares, not misled by his own vicious inclinations. His reflections are sweet, when compared with mine. And his wife, even since his estrangement, has been happier than the villain who seduced him from her.—There is a delightful serenity which accompanies suffering virtue, and renders it superior to temptation. Methought Mrs. Herbert, when she repulsed me, appeared more angelic than ever. Offended virtue sparkled in her eye, and glowed on her cheek.—Never was the cause of heaven so well supported.

I felt abashed.—I secretly acknowledged the superiority of goodness;—yet, as if animated by some spirit, an enemy to mankind, I wished to debase her character, and to render guilty, the object of my adoration. Her good angel prevailed—she flew from me.

I have injured Herbert, but I cannot forgive him for knowing me, nor for being happier than myself.

So *you* once declined turning your sword upon him, *for reasons too tedious to mention.* Rather, Brumpton, too obvious to require to be mentioned. Thou art a conceited fellow.—What! I imagine you had a desire to inspire me with a good opinion of your courage. It will not do, Captain—but how I trifle.

Herbert certainly intends to reform, and his wife will receive him. I have hastened my own, in the endeavour to complete his ruin.—Fool!—Blockhead!—Madman!

You have also mentioned another cause of despair.—Yes! I was the seducer of Miss Juliet R— —. She was promised, you know, to Lord M— —. I handed her one night from the play to a chair I had hired, and carried her to a proper house for her reception. Her father was at an estate in a distant country, and had entrusted her to the care of an aunt, negligent of her charge, and corrupt in her principles. Miss R— — was a very amiable woman. I hoped her love for me would have secured her secrecy; but on her vowing revenge, I would not permit her to return home.

Whether, in my absence, she was accessary to her own death, or whether the wretch with whom I placed her, learning her rank, dispatched her to avoid discovery, I know not, but I received the former account.

I believe you were before only imperfectly acquainted with this affair.—Lord M— — was then on his travels. He lately returned, and I heard was determined to find out the author of Miss R— —'s misfortunes. Her father has made many fruitless enquiries. To my servant I must attribute this discovery. He has decamped, after robbing me of whatever valuables he could collect.

I *must* pursue your advice, and shall take post horses early in the morning, for I have no time to lose. I shall not join you at Portsmouth till you are ready to sail, and then in disguise. I shall hire servants entirely unacquainted with me, and assume a borrowed name, by which means I hope to escape without observation.

I have written to my uncle, confided to him the trust of the whole sad affair, and intreated him to solicit my pardon, with promises of entire reformation.—The old man is not hard-hearted.—I am the hope of his family, and I flatter myself, he will even unlock the strong box to facilitate my return.

Courage, Brumpton! I shall revisit England. In the mean time, (for this is rather a distant prospect,) you shall share my purse and wardrobe.—I have converted what furniture my servant left me, into money, and begged of my uncle to be regular in his remittances.— You and I may be useful to each other.

* * * * *

I fear I have been too long a villain, to commence a life of virtue.— And I am too young to reform.—Is not repentance the last act of life?—O Brumpton, shall I own I almost envy thy insipid state? I have proved that the success of all those contrivances, on which my boasted superiority was founded, has only shewn the inefficacy of guilty stratagem to procure happiness.

What horrors filled my mind, when in my violent fever, I revolved my past crimes, and feared future punishment!—Despair of life made me consider the consequences of death!—In these hours of solitude, heavy reflections will not be banished.—I dare not fly to company for relief, and the wicked have few real friends.—My most intimate acquaintance are those from whom I have most to fear.

You, Brumpton, whom I have considered as the mere tool of my vile purposes, I am now convinced are a happier being than myself.— You have not been enslaved by vice, but seduced by folly.—How does conviction impress this truth on my soul, that superior talents are only properly exerted when they render us useful members of society.—Our abuse of intended blessings, is the certain cause of our condemnation.

Believe me, I would willingly relinquish every lucrative possession, every ambitious prospect, every gay delight, to be enabled to recollect one virtuous action, the remembrance of which would cast a ray of comfort on my benighted soul, and render my exile less dreadful!

The disorder of my mind affects my body—sometimes my veins feel scorched by a consuming fire, at others, chilled by the frost of bitter despondency.—I am afraid of laying aside my pen, lest a more offensive weapon should present itself.—Yet I can write no more.

* * * * *

I have scribbled all night—Methinks a dawn of joy breaks in to dissipate my gloom. Though I can receive no satisfaction from a retrospect, my future conduct may be an improvement on the past, and open before me a more enlightening prospect.—Though I am old in vice, my age permits me to hope for many added years. Continued excesses might have been the means of abridging, but regularity may prolong, and teach me to enjoy them.

I had an excellent father, but he died too soon for my advantage. My mother lost her life in giving me birth.—Brumpton! I *will* endeavour no further to degenerate from their examples.

My banishment, which till this moment I considered as a misfortune, I now hope may contribute to my greatest, most lasting happiness.— I shall leave all those companions, whose examples influenced, whose contrivances assisted, and whose contempt might have intimidated me.

For you, I know your heart is so ductile, it will pursue with pleasure the path I tread.—Pardon me, for drawing you into one which would have terminated in your destruction.—You want only resolution to practise every duty.—You will forsake your follies, when you consider them as an introduction to guilt.

I have been a veteran in overcoming the difficulties that opposed the triumphs of vice. I am now convinced, he only is a true hero, who conquers the obstacles which impede his advancement in virtue.— As a proof of my sincerity, I have written to Sally Marston's brother, acknowledging myself to have been her seducer. I have also sent her a letter, and inclosed a draught on my uncle for £500. to be paid into her hands on her return to her brother. Would to God I could make restitution of her fame and virtue; and restore to many injured innocents, the honour, of which, by repeated perjuries, I have deprived them.

You will imagine, perhaps, my change is too sudden to be permanent. I shall neither be surprized nor displeased at such a suspicion, for though (according to an excellent and admired writer whom I once dipped into) "To know ourselves diseased, is half our cure," yet Rowe was a more competent judge of human nature, when he says,

> "*Habitual* evils change not on a *sudden*
> "But *many* days *must pass*, and *many* sorrows
> "Conscious remorse and anguish *must* be felt,
> "To curb desire, to break the stub- born will,
> "And work a second nature in the soul
> "Ere virtue can resume the place she lost;
> "'Tis else *dissimulation*."

But, as I observed before, I shall have no enemy soliciting without, to assist the seducer within.—Besides, I feel diffident of my own strength, at the same time that I determine to exert it.—I will if possible

> — — — — — —"conquer difficulties
> By daring to oppose them. Sloth and folly
> Shiver and shrink at sight of toil and danger,
> And make th' impossibility they fear."

But the horses are at the door.—I have hired for the direct contrary road to that I propose taking.—This will elude any search.

Adieu! Brumpton.—As you have been the assistant of vice, be now the promoter of virtue, and aid with your counsels and example, the good resolutions of

The Wife; or, Caroline Herbert

Your sincere friend,

WILTON.

LETTER LXXII.

To Mrs. Berkeley.

THANKS to Heaven, dear Madam, my sister is out of danger. After I had sent away my hasty scrawl, she appeared to be more composed, and wrote a letter to my brother, which she carefully concealed under her pillow.

The fatigue of writing, of her emotions from the subject of her letter, occasioned a relapse, which greatly alarmed us all.—I concluded we had lost this most excellent of women, and gave her letter to my brother in an agony of distress.—Ah! what were his sufferings.—She at length recovered from the swoon which bore so strong an image of death, and sunk into a gentle slumber.

On her awaking the next morning, she gave us the delightful assurance, that she felt far less pain than she had yesterday suffered, and much recruit of strength.—As I was seated by her bed side, "My dear," said she "I thought yesterday I had but few hours to live, and I could not leave the world without addressing a few words to the partner of my soul, which endeavoured to console him. He loves me more than ever.—With what tenderness does he fear to lose me!"

My blushes betrayed my precipitance.—"I am sorry he has seen the letter," resumed she, "it affected him. Ah! my Lucy, to be summoned so soon after our blessed reconciliation, it was a most severe trial:—but that gracious Being, who knoweth whereof we are made, who saw it was good for me to be in trouble, supported me under affliction."

My brother, who had left the room just before she awaked, now returned. He flew to the bedside: he saw the alteration in her looks. She threw her arms round his neck.—"My husband!" "My Caroline!" was all, either could utter.—Well did they verify Shakespeare's observation, "I were but little happy, if I could say how much."

The Wife; or, Caroline Herbert

After some minutes speechless ecstacy, my brother raising his eyes to heaven, exclaimed, "Almighty, ever-gracious Being, wilt thou restore to me this best of women? Wilt thou permit her to guide my every future step?"

"Ah! my best beloved," resumed she, "may I endeavour to render added life a blessing to you, to others, and to myself!"—She was fearful of his saying more. "We will not talk," pursued she, "only give me your hand and sit by me."—She pressed his hand to her lips.—The conscious tear stole from his eye. I led to indifferent subjects.

* * * * *

My sister was drest this morning, when I went into her chamber, and looked as if almost restored to health. Little Charles was with her, and she fervently returned thanks to Heaven, for his and her own preservation. How is even this most excellent of human beings elevated by sufferings!—My brother must be a convert to the most exalted virtues.—I am certain he feels for her an heightened admiration, love, and esteem.

Mr. and Mrs. Henry Berkeley arrived in town the evening after the sad accident, and we want only to be with you to be the happiest of human beings.

Since my sister's recovery, Mrs. Bride had been wonderfully jocose.—"She cannot bear," she says, "that I should wear the willow garland, when Hymen has woven so many myrtle wreaths to surround the brows of my friends."

She rallies me about a gentleman who has visited here lately, and who, she is sure, though he professes little, means much. Perhaps there may be some slight attachment, but for my own part, I have been so engrossed by the situation of this dear family, that I have found no leisure for other thoughts.—Have I, dear Madam, enkindled any spark of friendly curiosity?—I know you love me, you wish me happy.—This gentleman is Sir Henry Romney; he has long been acquainted with Lord Wilton, but instead of sharing, always cautioned him against his excesses. He is, I suppose, fifteen years older than myself, but he is very estimable, very amiable, and—but when he is explicit, I will be more communicative.

I am, dear Madam,

Your now happy,

and ever affectionate

LUCIA HERBERT.

LETTER LXXIII.

To Charles Herbert, Esq.

ACCEPT, dear Sir, my most cordial congratulations on the recovery of Mrs. Herbert. I am certain the excellence of your principles and disposition must, on the prospect of your suffering so severe a loss as of this best of wives, and of women, have operated with their full force towards the completion of a perfect reunion.

Let the strictest confidence ever subsist between you, and, my dear Sir, do not think me impertinent for offering advice. Permit me to recommend to you a duty, which alone can secure you in the practice of every other religious obligation. I mean that of constant family and private prayer.

Ah! how often do we experience that we must be deprived of the blessings of Heaven, to become truly sensible of their value. Whilst a constant succession of bounties flows in upon us, we expect a repetition of them without an endeavour to deserve them; and what ought to augment, destroys our thankfulness and gratitude. When we receive a *single act* of friendship from *men*, we are eager to return the obligation, or at least to pay our grateful acknowledgments, whilst the *repeated*, the *inexhaustible favours* of the Deity are frequently received without observation, and therefore without thanks.

On you, my dear Mr. Herbert, the mercies of Providence have been very liberally bestowed. Forget not to adore the divine source of every blessing, and let no earthly attachment weaken your aspirations after a glorious eternity. Remember there is not so strong a defence against vice, as *constant prayer!* The fervent prayer "of a righteous man, availeth much."—If you would preserve in your children and servants a regard to their several duties, be regular in your *family prayers*. Let *your example*, as well as *your precepts*, influence their practice.

I would be no means recommend forms of prayer which would fatigue by their length. It is in general necessary to begin with some particular form, even in our private supplications, or we shall become unsteady in the performance of this duty; but different situations, dissimilar dispositions, require varied modes of address to God, for the peculiar virtues necessary to each state and frame of mind. The Deity regards not the length of the address, but the sincerity and fervour of the supplicant. I would choose such prayers as shew our penitence for offences, our dependence on God, and gratitude for his mercies.—He has appointed for us the means of grace, and from the use of these alone, through the merits of a Redeemer and Mediator, can we derive our hopes of glory.

Nothing but a *constant sense* of an *omniscient eye, can preserve us steady in our duty* at all *times,* in *all places,* and on *all occasions,* can influence our *intentions,* excite our *wishes,* and animate our *endeavours* to *please God in every action of our lives.*

Will you, my dear Sir, indulge me with your permission to introduce my Henrietta to Mrs. Herbert? We shall return into Oxfordshire within a few days, and I cannot be satisfied without laying the basis of a personal intercourse with your amiable and respectable family,

I am, with sincere esteem,

Your obliged and affectionate

ROBERT FOREST.

LETTER LXXIV.

To Mrs. Berkeley.

Dear Madam,

MY heart overflows with joy, and gratitude. We are happier than ever. The penitent has been forgiven, and love and harmony have resumed their united dominion.

When I entered the room, this morning, my sister's features glowed with peculiar animation, and joy seemed to have taken possession of her soul. She arose with a smile of ineffable sweetness, and folded me to her heart. I understood the embrace.—My brother took my hand.—"My angelic Caroline," said he, "has forgiven her wanderer, and he must likewise be reconciled to you." I wept, while I gave him my hand, and for some moments we were all silent.

I thought it was in my power to increase their happiness. I ran to the nursery, took little Charles in my arms, and re-entered the apartment of his fond parents.—The sight of the child strongly affected my brother. He cast down his eyes with a conscious embarrassment, but soon, gazing on the dear babe, he seemed to be forgetful of our presence.

My sister wept.—"I fear," said she, "you have affected him too much. How steadily he fixes his eyes on the child!"—I drew nearer to him:—he threw his arms around me, and the sweet infant, and burst into tears.

My sister was overcome with the scene.—She sunk into a chair. Her cheek was pale with agitation, and I saw her fainting. My brother also observed her altered countenance. He eagerly flew to her, caught her in his arms, and sustained her declining head on his breast. She recovered; the colour revisited her cheek.

At this moment, a servant entered, and presented her with a letter. She did not know the hand, but on opening the letter, gratified benevolence shone on her expressive countenance.

It came from one who had been a mistress of Lord Wilton, and who, by his instigation, had endeavoured to persuade my sister of my brother's repeated guilt. Her conjugal tenderness, and penetrating judgment, rejected the poison. She even promised to assist the poor weak instrument of Wilton's baseness, and to rescue her from indigence, if she would avoid vice.

It is impossible to describe the emotions which were depicted on the countenances of the reunited pair. My sister, whilst reading the letter, could not forbear glancing a look sometimes at my brother; the fear of giving him pain, suffused her cheeks with blushes, whilst her eyes expressed the tender sympathy of her heart.

My brother's curiosity was expressed by an humiliating apprehension.—At last, in an accent tremulous with the agitation of his mind,—"Has not my Caroline," said he, in a faultering voice, "received a confirmation of my guilt?"

"No, best beloved of my heart," answered she, "it rather bears testimony to your undeviating will.—Read the letter, my dear Mr. Herbert, and do you read it, sister, and join with me in blessing Heaven for the penitence it strongly delineates." She then withdrew into an adjoining room to write an answer.

Be pleased here to read the letter of the poor penitent.

"*To Mrs. Herbert.*

"You promised, Madam, to relieve my self-inflicted sufferings, if I gave no new cause of disapprobation, and to contribute to her ease, who had endeavoured to destroy yours.

"Alas! how am I humbled by comparison with your excellence. Lately I was a proud, vain mortal, proud of a "set of features and complexion," which exposed me to temptations too powerful for my weak virtue.—Ah! how far do you outshine me even in exterior.—I was vain of an understanding I had perverted, and elevated by trappings, for which I had paid the guilty price of innocence and reputation.

"Lord Wilton was my seducer. He it was who bribed me by his deceitful tenderness, to impose upon Mr. Herbert by a feigned tale of distress. Only Lord Wilton and I were guilty. Shame to my sex!—O! Madam, let me bury my guilt in silence. Spare me, best of women!

"Assure yourself, Madam, depend on my most solemn protestations, I never saw Mr. Herbert except that time; that his momentary forgetfulness was immediately expiated by contrition. How could I, after this proof of his unalienated affection for you, endeavour to withdraw your's from him? I abhor myself for the attempt; I admire and reverence you beyond expression; but I need not become a petitioner for your bounty.

"Heaven be praised! Lord Wilton gives hopes of his reformation. He has not only restored into my brother's hands the little fortune I resigned to him, but even added to it. I accept this present as a proof of his repentance, and as an exercise of my humility.

"My brother, with a kindness as unexpected as unmerited, has received me into his house and favour. His behaviour is so inexpressibly tender, that it increases my shame and my penitence, and sets virtue in the most amiable light.

"Lord Wilton is gone abroad.—I rejoice in this circumstance, as it gives me more time to disengage my heart, and fortify my mind.

"Will you, Madam, deign to assist with your advice a poor weak creature, who is diffident of herself. A line from your hand will confirm and strengthen every good resolution, and enable me to put them in practice.

"Permit me, with the most grateful sense of your goodness, and the most humble consciousness of my own offences, to thank you for that truly christian benevolence, by which you exalt me to hope, and encourage me to attempt, a thorough regulation of manners.

"Ah! join your prayers with mine. The address of so pure a heart will be accepted at the throne of mercy, and, I hope, draw down a blessing on the head of

Your ever grateful

and eternally obliged

SARAH MARSTON."

My brother wept over the letter, and when he had finished the third perusal of it, his uplifted eyes thanked Heaven for the penitence of the writer. I congratulated him on the prospect of Lord Wilton's reformation. He again raised his eyes to Heaven.

My sister soon after joined us. She gave my brother her answer. She lifted his hand to her lips, and again retired. I inclose a transcript of her letter.

"*To Miss Marston.*

"You accuse yourself, dear Miss Marston, of having been the cause of my uneasiness. Give me leave to assure you, I have received from your present sentiments a very high degree of satisfaction.

"I will not attempt to palliate what you condemn, but from a consciousness of my own frailties, I have learned to pity those whose conduct I cannot approve. I am convinced that it is more difficult to reform than to persevere; and that angels rejoice in the conversion of offenders.

"You solicit my encouragement and support. I readily grant it. You may task my power to its utmost extent, but depend not on *human aid.* Constantly and fervently supplicate the Almighty that his providence may be your guard. Remember, dear Miss Marston, you have not only to attend to a *regulation of manners*, but to a *reformation of principles*. My constant and fervent prayers shall be offered for you.

I rejoice for your sake, in Lord Wilton's absence, but though your greatest danger is removed, endeavour before you re-enter the world, to fortify your mind against its delusions.

"The world's infectious, few bring back at eve
"Immaculate the manners of the morn;
"Something we thought, is blotted; we resolv'd,
"Is shaken; we renounc'd, returns again,
"Each salutation may slide in a sin
"Unthought before, or fix a former stain.
"Present example gets within our guard.
"A slight, a single glance
"And shot at random, often has brought home
"A sudden fever to the throbbing heart,
"Of envy, rancour, or impure desire."

"The remembrance of a known error tends to exclude presumption, as it proves the necessity of a stricter subsequent conduct; but let not humility occasion a dejection of spirit equally prejudicial to the interests of religion.

"Deserve the good opinion of the world and you will most probably in time regain it; but let not human approbation be the motive, nor consider it as the reward of your actions.

"Endeavour to *sanctify every* action by an *intention* of *pleasing God,* who sees the heart, and will reward the glorious purpose, even where it *cannot* be ripened into performance.

"In every circumstance of your future life, where I can promote your happiness, I beg you will remember you have a real and constant friend in

CAROLINE HERBERT."

I will not attempt to paint the tender scene which succeeded.

My brother is exalted in my affection and esteem. My sister,—but I should wrong her excellence by an endeavour to praise it. May their happiness be uninterrupted, and may you, dear Madam, long, long live to enjoy this blessed reunion, is the fervent prayer of

Your obliged and affectionate

LUCIA HERBERT.

LETTER LXXV.

To Mrs. Herbert.

My dear Child,

I COULD in my letters to you, suppress my melancholy participation in your grief, because I would not injure the dignity of your conduct, but when I know you are acquainted with the informations I have received, and that you experience the most delightful change, I cannot forbear to join the warm congratulations of a mother, with other of your truly affectionate, yet less interested friends.

What have you suffered! And how nobly have you acted!—And are you well, are you quite well, my dearest daughter?—Heaven be praised for your preservation. Ah! what anguish have I endured, lest I should survive the darling of my heart!

Mr. Herbert is again my beloved son. He has entitled himself to the love and esteem of every good mind.—Your happiness is restored.— Your brother's is completed.—Come, my dear children, come and render mine perfect—I long to embrace the sweet image of your perfections, and to thank the friendly Miss Herbert. You and they, share my love, blessing, and affectionate respects.

Your sufferings and your virtues, my Caroline, have endeared you still more to the ever-fond heart, of

Your affectionate mother,

ELIZABETH BERKELEY.

LETTER LXXVI.

To Mrs. Berkeley.

Dear and honoured Madam,

THE accident which befel my beloved sister, suspended all our joys on the happiest event of my life.—Never did my Clara or I experience so violent a shock as we felt on the receipt of Miss Herbert's letter.

We hastened to town; our fears were increased, my brother's wretchedness was inexpressible. All was silent, unutterable anguish.—But thanks to an ever-gracious Providence, our past woes serve only to increase our present delights.

My brother sometimes sighs.—Reflection wounds him, but it has produced the most salutary effects. He is more endeared than ever to us all.—It is with exultation and gratitude I can now assure you, my sister is almost as happy as she is good. How have the mother, the daughter, and the wife, suffered; but the *Christian*, God be praised! the *Christian* triumphed, in every character. The bloom of health has revisited her cheek, and beauty re-animates every feature.

My Clara has made me the happiest of men! O delightful reflection! she is ever and only mine. Your natural tenderness will be gratified by these communications, and the happiness of your children be completed, when they can receive your personal congratulations and blessings. In a few days I hope to present to the best of mothers the daughter of her wishes, in the chosen and beloved wife of

her ever dutiful,

grateful, and affectionate Son,

HENRY BERKELEY.

LETTER LXXVII.

To Mrs. Berkeley.

AFTER all my flippancies and levities, I think myself happy, dear and honoured Madam, that you have deemed me not unworthy to be admitted into a family, where the life of each individual forms an example for my imitation.—Never had I so awakening a call upon my humility, as since I have seriously compared myself with the Herberts and the Berkeleys.

I congratulated myself yesterday, and condoled with my spouse. A Mr. and Miss Forest paid Mr. and Mrs. Herbert a visit. The old gentleman is not a fit subject for a gay pen. He commands my reverence and respect.

The young lady is most strikingly agreeable. Ah! luckless event, Berkeley, said I, "if you had not been fettered, what a blissful choice might you have made!" The man returned a bride-groom like answer. He is satisfied with me at present. I will endeavour to deserve that he shall always be so.

With the name of Woodford, I hope I have bidden adieu to folly. I am now incorporated amongst the worthies. Never may I disgrace the respectable name I now bear! I am impatient, dearest Madam, to throw myself at your feet, and to be acknowledged by you as

Your dutiful

and affectionate daughter,

CLARA BERKELEY.

LETTER LXXVIII.

To Mrs. Berkeley.

Dearest, ever honoured Madam,

IT is impossible to convey the effusions of gratitude, joy, and love, with which my heart is filled.—My mind is no longer a prey to corroding grief. My health is restored. My prospects in this life are enlarged. My child is unhurt!

Shall I soon see you again? O! best of parents, shall I be clasped again to your maternal bosom? A few days since, I dared not to indulge the hope, but my heart now throbs quick with joyful expectation.

I wrote a last farewell.—I breathed the emotions of my heart; that heart which felt all the tortures of approaching separation. Yet I looked forward to a blissful reunion. I never considered my dear husband as merely the partner of this transitory scene, but as an help-mate to an eternity of happiness. It has pleased God to grant me a longer date of life. Whilst I am truly thankful for the blessing, I will endeavour to make it a lesson of humility. I am not yet qualified for an admittance into that state, where, founded on faith in the merits of a Redeemer, superiority of virtue alone can exalt to a pre-eminence of happiness.

A thousand thanks to you, dearest Madam, for your sympathetic tenderness. You forgave my silence. Ah! little did I imagine you to be acquainted with my misfortune. But banished be all further retrospects.—I never lost Mr. Herbert's esteem nor love; his heart now fully repays the tenderness, the anxiety of mine. He acts not from the present influence of passion; his conduct is not merely the effect of my unrepining submission: he is restored by a sense of duty, the force of Christian principles.

The Wife; or, Caroline Herbert

"The consequence of my dissipation," says the best beloved of my heart, "was the neglect of family and private prayer, and that neglect the cause of my farther deviations. Never, my Caroline, never let us omit to offer our heart-felt supplications at the throne of grace; supplications which prove at once, our insufficiency and our sure dependence. How weak indeed are human endeavours, unless supported by divine assistance."

* * * * *

My sister Berkeley, has in her lively way introduced Mr. and Miss Forest to your acquaintance. I hope you will be a personal sharer in our satisfaction on the acquisition of two such friends. He is one of the most respectable of men. She, one of the most amiable of women.

My sister Herbert tells me, she has slightly hinted to you Sir Henry Romney's attachment to her. I believe he deserves her. Can I do more justice to his merit? Her heart is really touched. The similarity of our sentiments on the subject of love has drawn closer that silken tye of amity, which has long "entwined our hearts in one," and my sister Berkeley forms the triple band.

* * * * *

This moment my dear Mr. Herbert tells me, we may hope to be with you on Wednesday. My little Charles will smile his joy on seeing you. My beloved husband fears he shall not be re-admitted to that share of your affection he once enjoyed. Ah! my dear parent, he shall not indulge a suspicion injurious to you and to himself.

Oh! Madam, how delightful are the rewards of duty, even in this life! How amply are all my sufferings repaid. As Christianity has a resource in the most afflicting incidents of mortality, so its delights are heightened by the certainty of their future increase and perpetual duration.

Animated by the enjoyment of temporal happiness, and the prospect of eternal felicity, I can truly subscribe myself,

Your happy, dutiful,

and affectionate daughter,

CAROLINE HERBERT.

THE END.

Lightning Source UK Ltd.
Milton Keynes UK
02 July 2010

156388UK00002B/149/P